A TIME TO DANCE

Deborah thinks that nothing exciting happens in wartime Bristol. But then the Americans arrive, preparing to fight in occupied Europe. And for Deborah, everything changes. She finds excitement when she meets Warren and falls in love. But her romantic dreams are shattered when her father sends her away to live with her aunt in Exmouth. And more heartbreak follows when she feels forced to seek refuge in London. At the end of the war — can she ever find happiness again?

EILEEN STAFFORD

A TIME
TO DANCE

Complete and Unabridged

LINFORD
Leicester

First published in Great Britain in 2008

First Linford Edition
published 2009

British Library CIP Data

Stafford, Eileen
    A time to dance.—Large print ed.—
Linford romance library
    1. Love stories
    2. Large type books
    I. Title
    823.9'2 [F]

    ISBN 978–1–84782–531–5

Published by
F. A. Thorpe (Publishing)
Anstey, Leicestershire
Set by Words & Graphics Ltd.
Anstey, Leicestershire
Printed and bound in Great Britain by
T. J. International Ltd., Padstow, Cornwall

1

Deborah Jenkins stood outside the Headmistress's office and stared apprehensively at the light above the door. When it flashed it would be her cue to enter. She pulled at her red gymslip and fiddled nervously with the girdle around her waist. She hoped that her hair, with its two short plaits, was tidy, and that her black stockings weren't too wrinkled. Her suspenders would never keep them up properly.

What was the dragon about to say to her? Why had she received the dreaded summons this morning immediately after register? Her homework was in on time, she hadn't strung her felt hat on the handlebars of her bicycle, but had held it firmly on her head even while freewheeling down the hill into school, and she hadn't been late. What then could it be?

She felt hot colour rush to her face when she thought of last Saturday night, and the Saturday before that and . . . Surely word couldn't have reached the school? She had been careful, had changed at her friend's house, and the outfit she had worn was surely a perfect disguise. No-one could have recognised her.

The light above the door started to flash ominously. She knocked and tiptoed in. Miss Weston was sitting behind her desk. She looked up and frowned.

'I am afraid that I have the gravest accusation to put before you, Deborah,' she said. 'I have been told that you have been seen on three occasions frequenting a very doubtful venue in the town. That you have been wearing lipstick and flaunting yourself in a manner that brings disgrace to our school, and to your parents.'

Deborah stood silently before her accuser and knew that she couldn't deny the terrible and wonderful things she had done. Her parents were unsuspecting. Three times she had told them that she was staying with her friend, that it was just an innocent weekend, that she would be studying most of the time. School Certificate was looming and Stella, whose father was a teacher, was very respectable.

They had a lot of books which would help her with her work she had said. Stella had taken School Certificate last year, had passed with two distinctions and four credits.

'She helps me with my homework,' Deborah told them. She had her fingers crossed behind her back as she spoke hoping that the half-truth would be forgiven. She was certainly going to stay with Stella, and just occasionally she asked her for help with a maths problem. That made it seem slightly better!

But the Americans were in town weren't they, with their money, their glamour, their nylons and their wild music. She thought of the whirling excitement of the jive, of Warren with his golden close-cut curls, twirling her over his arm, her skirt fanning to her waist, showing the delicate filmy nothingness of the nylons he had given her and which clothed her legs with sensuous delight. They were a world away from the thick lisle things she wore to school.

Standing now in front of her headmistress her crime assumed vast proportions. She hung her head in shame for her deceit and studied the intricate pattern of the carpet beneath her feet. 'I've been to a social a few times,' she whispered, trying to make it sound respectable. 'On Saturday nights.' She wished she could have said, 'Church Social.'

'And with whom did you go?'

Here she was on safer ground. Her friend, Stella Brown, was a girl she met regularly on Sundays at church.

She was not a pupil at this prestigious grammar school. Stella was older and more worldly wise.

Her scholarly father was a widower and knew little of what his daughter did, so the girls met at her home, giggled, experimented with make up and clothes, mostly Stella's clothes, for she was working now and had a little more money to spare.

Stella was a great contriver and a skilled needle woman too, and together they rigged themselves up every Saturday night. Navy blue knickers and liberty bodices gave way to flimsy items sometimes made of parachute silk. Heavy lace-up shoes were replaced with those once worn by Stella's long dead mother, strappy sparkling affairs from the twenties.

'I was with my friend from church,' Deborah said. That at least sounded respectable.

'Name please?'

She hesitated. Miss Weston held absolute power over the girls in her school, but Stella was not one of them.

'Stella Brown,' she said quietly. 'She was never here, Miss Weston. She was at St Margaret's.'

The headmistress sniffed. 'And you have also been seen out in the town with . . . ' Now it was her turn to hesitate. The words *Yank* or *GI* could never pass her lips. 'With our American allies,' she added piously. 'They are no doubt brave and admirable young men, but when they are here, naturally they expect . . . ' Here she paused again and breathed deeply. 'They expect to enjoy themselves, but not, I repeat, not, with girls from this school. You are all too young and would be too easily led.'

Another pause and Deborah raised her head and looked at her prim headmistress and wondered if she could ever have known the amazing delights of whirling around a dance hall in the arms of a man like Warren. Oh no, of course not. The very idea was quite preposterous and if she were not feeling so frightened at this moment she could almost have giggled.

'This behaviour of yours will not do, Deborah,' Miss Weston went on. 'If you continue to make such a spectacle of yourself you will be expelled from this school. A grammar school education is a great privilege. You have your School Certificate exams to sit very shortly and you must give all your time to your studies. You are a clever girl.' Her tone moderated a little. 'Now go and let me hear no more of this despicable behaviour. Your parents will, of course, be informed.'

'Thank you, Miss Weston.' Deborah turned awkwardly, nearly tripping over one of her shoe laces. She groped for the door handle and let herself out. Once in the hall she paused and leaned against the wall. She thought with horror of Miss Weston's last sentence, 'Your parents will, of course, be informed.'

The horror of facing her father was too awful to contemplate. She had indeed been let off lightly by her school, but her parents were quite another matter.

And there was Warren. How could

she possibly give him up forever? She loved him with her whole heart and he was bringing fun and magic into her life. She wished she could go with him to some enchanted land where there was no school and no fighting.

The war would soon take him away of course. She often thought that the world of adults was a hostile and evil place and her innocent dancing and loving was surely preferable to all the hate and death that respectable grown-ups brought upon the world.

She walked slowly back to her class. Latin this morning. The teacher looked up and nodded as she went to her place. Miss Fenchurch had obviously been told. Deborah blushed, took out her books and found the page indicated on the blackboard. She saw nothing of the printed words at first. She could only see Warren's laughing eyes and smart uniform.

Then she started the translation. She did it automatically and without fault for this was her favourite subject. And when she had finished she laid down her pen and stared out of the window and remembered with trembling heart what she and Warren had done after the dancing and the fun. What could happen? She dare not ask. Even Stella would think she had been stupid and too easily led.

School dinners were usually awful, but today Deborah expected them to be even worse to match her mood. She'd have to force it down though however she felt. Miss Pringle, games and dinners, would never allow a girl to leave without an empty plate. There was a war on wasn't there? They had to be grateful for every mouthful, and all brought to them by our brave men risking their lives on the Atlantic convoys. It was mortal sin to leave even one sprout.

Deborah had herself joined the diggers and planters who had turned the front lawns of the school into a vast vegetable patch. Cabbage and potatoes hadn't to be brought from overseas so why did she have to eat every morsel? However no girl dared argue, and they all rebelliously stuffed stew or bubble and squeak into their reluctant mouths. But first of course there was always grace, sung stiffly to attention and in Latin.

As they shuffled into the dining hall, Maureen, Deborah's best school friend, whispered anxiously, 'What did she want you for? Good or bad?'

'Bad,' Deborah said. 'Tell you later.'

Miss Pringle glared at them and they all stood silently while the pianist struck up the first chords of the grace. As the ancient and beautiful words came to an end the girls climbed over the forms and Deborah looked at the large casserole at the end of the table. Chopped vegetables in cheese sauce.

'Vomit,' Maureen said cheerfully.

Deborah held her stomach. 'Don't! Please, Maureen, don't say that word.'

Maureen looked at her and grinned. 'What's the matter with you? That's what it looks like.'

The sun shone brightly on that Spring day in 1944 and after the horrors of the meal the girls were allowed twenty minutes to relax. Deborah and Maureen linked arms and walked down the drive towards the school gate. 'There's no-one listening now,' Maureen said. 'So come on. What have you done?'

'I've been out dancing with the Yanks.'

Maureen stopped and stared at her friend. 'Gosh, have you really? That's absolutely ripping.'

'No it's not. Someone has reported me. Mum and Dad thought I was doing homework at Stella's house. I met this particular one, Warren, and I've fallen in love with him. Well, I think I have. Honestly, Maureen, it's the most amazing thing that's ever happened to me and now . . . it has to finish for ever.'

Maureen gawped helplessly at her. 'So what'll you do?'

Deborah shrugged. 'It depends,' she

said. 'I don't want to talk about it.' How could she tell anyone what it was like? That it was the beginning of the world, the end of the world, that it was everything.

'That's mean,' Maureen said. 'I want to know what it's like, going with boys. Mum and Dad won't let me out of their sight. Even when we stayed with my gran in London I wasn't allowed past the front door on my own.'

'Don't say a word, will you?' Deborah was anxious now, wishing she had said nothing.

Maureen shrugged. 'Not if that's what you want, but I still think you're rotten not to tell me a few bits. And what about that cousin you were always talking about? Luke wasn't it?'

'I love him too,' Deborah replied. 'But I haven't seen him for ages, and anyway it's different. He's like a brother. Simon too. They've always been there. Until they both joined up of course.'

'OK, I'll keep your secret,' Maureen

said. 'You're my best friend.'

Harmony partly restored they walked back to the school building in silence, and to double history. History for goodness sake, the nineteenth century, the Repeal of the Corn Laws. What had all that to do with now, with Hitler striding across the world, with the bombs and the horror? But Deborah knew that she would probably get a distinction in history. She must put today out of her mind and concentrate on yesterday however hard that was. Worries about what she was to tell her parents would have to wait.

★ ★ ★

'So you have been deceiving us,' her mother said. Her eyes were puffy and red. She had obviously been crying. 'I never thought you could do such a thing, Deborah, and with your brains too.'

What had brains to do with it, Deborah wondered? How could brains stop you doing the very thing that all your being cried out to do? To be with Warren, to whirl madly around the dance floor with him in tune with that intoxicating music. And then afterwards? Well that was something else, something that now, suddenly, brought colour rushing to her cheeks, and a surge of shame and worry.

Yes, worry. Perhaps 'brains' might have stopped her being so stupid, she thought miserably. But hers had proved quite ineffectual. When it came to the crunch, body was more powerful than brains.

'You'll not be allowed to see Stella again,' her mother said. 'Your father has been round and talked to her dad. Poor man, he was as shocked as we were, and him with no wife to share the load and his son taken prisoner somewhere hundreds of miles away.'

She was sitting at her sewing machine, her feet quite still for a moment on the treadles. She was making a pair of curtains into a summer dress. These bright cotton drapes had once graced the front sitting room, but for some time now had been replaced by yards of blackout curtains which gloomily festooned every window in the house.

'But she's my friend,' Deborah wailed.

'She isn't your friend any more,' her mother said. 'You should have thought about that before you allowed her to lead you astray.'

Deborah dumped her satchel on the sturdy oak table that was placed squarely in the bay window, and unbuckled the straps.

Her mother glanced at the well thumbed books which slid out. 'It looks as if you've got enough homework for a month of Sundays,' she said. 'You can do it down here if you like while I finish this dress. I shan't be laying the table for another hour. I'm not saying any more about your escapades until your dad comes in. We'll see what he's got to say to you. He was very angry when he came for his dinner.' She looked at Deborah sadly. 'Why did you do it, love?' she said, more kindly now. 'Whatever made you lie to us, Debbie?'

Deborah hung her head in shame. As long as her mother was angry then she could be defiant, but gentleness made her feel really bad. 'Sorry, Mum. It was wrong I know, but it was all such fun.'

Pamela Jenkins got up from her seat and kissed Debbie freely. Then she smiled. 'Don't say that to your father,' she said. She shook her head and turned back to her work.

Deborah looked at her and wondered if there had been any fun in her mother's life long long ago, back in the twenties she supposed. She'd heard that they had dances then, that the girls were called bright young things. Had her mother ever been to one of those? It was hard to imagine.

She slumped down at the kitchen table and glanced at the jumble of exercise books and homework she had brought home.

How could she possibly sort out her school work if she had made such a mess of more important things?

'Come on, love,' her mother said. 'You get started and I'll make you and me a cup of tea. I made some carrot cake this morning.'

Deborah smiled at her mother and brushed back a tear. 'Thanks Mum, that'll be great.' Carrot cake was the panacea for everything, and even though a few moments ago she had felt that she couldn't eat a thing, she managed the moist piece of cake and felt momentarily better.

Then she thought of her father and shivered and wished she could escape to her bedroom, but this was the only room in the house with a fire. He came home from his office regularly every night on the 6 o'clock bus, and tonight, as she tried to concentrate on her homework she waited fearfully for the sound of his key in the lock.

She had never been frightened of her father before. She remembered those times early in the war when she had been younger, and she had been happy to seek the comfort of his arms as Mr Churchill gave his dramatic and sometimes frightening speeches on the wireless.

They would sit in the big red plush armchair beside the fire and listen to talk of blood, sweat and tears, and she had felt secure because she had been sure then that her father was a safe bulwark between her and the world. Her mother, also listening, just got on with her knitting and showed no fear either. But now it was different.

Her parents weren't on her side any more. They were against her, even her mother was unhappy about it. They had no understanding of this amazing thing that had happened to her. Did they understand what it was like to be in love for the very first time? She wished she could believe that they did, but it was too hard to imagine.

She heard the familiar sounds of her father hanging his trilby on one of the pegs on the hall-stand and then putting his coat on its hanger. He walked down the passage, his boots clanking on the stone tiles. She saw the door knob turn and then there he was standing in the doorway glaring at her. Her mother pecked his cheek nervously.

'Had a good afternoon, dear?' she asked deferentially. He ignored her and went over to the large plush armchair but instead of sitting down he turned his back to the fire and clasped his hands behind him.

'What's all this your mother has been telling me?' He barked the words out in a voice Deborah had seldom heard him use, certainly not to her.

She stared down at her books. 'I've been to a social with Stella,' she muttered.

'Social, my eye. A dance hall more like, with all those damned Yanks, and more than once too. I won't have it, my girl, not at your age, not at any age if I had my way. And you've deceived us, told us you were round with that no-good friend of yours. Her poor mother must be turning in her grave.'

She saw that he was trembling and for one moment she felt a pang of regret. 'I'm sorry, Daddy. I'm so sorry.' The words sprang to her lips, but even as she uttered them she knew that she didn't truly mean them.

'Sorry! What good is sorry, when you've caused your mother and me such pain and disappointment?' He turned his back to her and stood staring into the flames. 'You've made yourself a cheap hussy, and if you ever get yourself *in* the family way, my girl, then it's out of this house with you, and I shall never want to see your face again. Understand?'

She wanted to run to him, fling her arms around his firm upstanding back, hug him and be his little girl again. She wanted him to put everything right just as it was years ago but she stood there, staring unseeing at her maths exercise book open on the table, and hot tears began to trickle down her cheeks.

Supposing, just supposing the terrible thing her friends whispered about sometimes, the thing that followed being too free with a man, supposing that happened to her? Warren would go off to war and . . . she couldn't imagine the horror of such a terrible fate for herself and for him.

'Clear those books away and lay the table for your mother,' her father thundered. He had recovered himself and his grief was replaced by anger. 'I want my tea.'

2

School now was terrible, and coming home each afternoon was even worse. Every day her heart sank when she turned the corner into the long straight road where she lived. Her parents' house was right in the middle and as she neared it she would stop pedalling and allow the bicycle to freewheel slowly until she reached number 93 with it's high privet hedge.

There was no gate. It had been requisitioned long ago to make Spitfires, revealing the gleaming brass step at the front door. Her mother polished it vigorously each morning with Brasso, and Deborah had to lift her heavy black bike carefully over the step so that it didn't leave any mud. Although this was a fairly spacious house, it stood in a terrace and everything and everyone had to come through the front door.

The bike had to be propped against the wall in the passage with a cloth over it so that it should not dirty the wallpaper, and when the coal man came with his delivery of 30 heavy sacks over his grimy shoulder, then her mother would put newspapers all down the passage and old dust sheets over the furniture in the kitchen.

Behind the long row of houses was an orphanage that had been occupied by different divisions of the forces ever since the children had been evacuated, and just now there were the Yanks. Their presence so close to his home made her father even more bad tempered, but every time Deborah saw them over the wall at the bottom of the garden she was reminded of Warren.

His division was quartered farther away, on the outskirts of the town and she hadn't seen him for ages. The Easter holidays had come and gone, and now it was the summer term. Deborah guessed that soon there would be a great battle in Hitler's Europe and her heart was terrified for Warren. He would be part of it and she would never see him again once that started.

Her father had started reading the newspaper aloud at breakfast again. For a time, after he had been so angry with her, he had stopped this habit and they ate their porridge in gloomy silence, but now something like normality had returned. Perhaps he had forgiven her? She wasn't sure.

One morning he shuffled the pages about angrily. He was eating one of their precious eggs, spooning the yolk carefully into his mouth. He glared at the page he had selected. 'Forty-seven British and Allied airmen have been shot after escaping from their prison camp,' he read. He pursed his lips in disgust and a frown spread across his forehead.

Deborah seldom commented on these news items, but her father's words always made her heart jump with fear for the men in her life who were all caught up in this awful war. Cousin

Luke, Simon, and now Warren. She wanted them all safe and sound and at home!

One day later that week, a satisfied grin spread over her father's features as he read. 'It looks like our boys are doing well over there,' he announced. 'Monte Casino.'

'That's Italy, isn't it?' her mother said. 'Please God, I hope Luke is safe. Sarah wrote that she thought he was somewhere in the South.'

Pamela sighed and poured another cup of tea for herself. 'Well,' she said, 'Simon's out of it in that Japanese prison camp.'

Deborah looked at her mother and father and kept her own thoughts to herself. The war was just too awful. She wished she could forget about it and just get on with her life, but she had heard terrible stories about the Japanese camps. She kept these horrors to herself too, and said nothing.

Her mother seldom read the papers and probably was better kept in ignorance. She wished her father hadn't started reading the newspapers to them every morning again. She couldn't help thinking of Warren each time he pointed out some new victory or defeat. But the more she heard the more her feelings of rebellion increased. Surely, with life itself and the future so uncertain, it was best to take every bit of happiness wherever you could find it?

Stella was her only hope of ever seeing Warren again. She worked in the grocer's shop on the corner on Saturdays to make a little pocket money, and that was the only way the two girls could meet now. Much of the family's rations had to be collected from this shop and Deborah's Saturday job was, conveniently, to fetch them.

'You've got to arrange something,' Deborah pleaded the next Saturday morning. 'I must see him again, Stella. He'll be going away to fight soon. There's things going on. He might be killed.'

Stella looked doubtful. 'Your dad came to see my dad the other evening and there was a great row. If we're seen together I don't know what'll happen.'

'We don't need to be seen together,' Deborah said desperately. 'You could tell Warren what's happened and fix something up couldn't you?'

Stella shrugged and turned her attention to the old lady who was impatiently waiting for her groceries. When the small basket was filled and the four shillings and sixpence handed over and stowed away in the till she turned back to Deborah, took her ration books and started to gather up the order.

She weighed out the sugar and a tiny piece of cheese before saying any more. There was a queue of curious shoppers waiting behind. 'Dad won't let me go to the dances either now,' she whispered. 'But I'll see what I can do. I know someone who does. I'll tell you next Saturday.'

'Thanks a million, Stella,' Deborah

said. 'I'll give you a bit of my sweet ration next week.' The two girls grinned at each other and Deborah wondered if she and Stella could ever be true friends again. Perhaps one day when they were grown up and could do what they liked they'd meet and laugh and have fun together; after the war! How wonderful that would be!

But for the moment Deborah had to be content with this short snatched conversation over the ration books, and perhaps, wonderful thought, with a secret meeting with Warren if Stella could manage to arrange it.

The following Saturday brought the great news. As Stella filled Deborah's basket and took the money, she whispered, 'On the Downs, your special place, after school on Monday!'

'You're wonderful,' Deborah whispered.

'That remains to be seen,' Stella commented in a sceptical voice. 'Just don't do anything daft, Debbie. He'll be gone soon and . . . ' Deborah cut her friend short. She walked out of the shop as demurely as she could, smiled to one or two of the ladies standing in the queue, and hoped no-one had heard any of those whispered words.

She knew that the Americans would soon disappear, might never think of their English conquests again, but Warren was different from the others. She was quite sure that he was! She tried to think only of being in Warren's arms once more.

She wanted to skip home instead of walking, but the rations in her basket were too precious, and as she walked slowly along the pavement her mind began to fill with more solemn thoughts. The enormity of what was happening to her and the horrors that were probably awaiting Warren in the fighting to come were too awful to contemplate.

Then there was the thought of her parents' wrath if they should know that she had deceived them again. She shivered in apprehension as she unpacked the basket onto the kitchen table when she reached home.

But her mother was more interested in the small amounts of food with which she had to feed the three of them than in any suspected liaisons of her daughter. 'Not much here to last us a week,' she said gloomily, and Deborah breathed a sigh of relief. Her mother knew that Stella worked in Bendle's Grocery Store on Saturdays, but she gave no sign that the girls might have met and talked. There were no difficult questions asked.

'It's your birthday on Monday,' she said in a more cheerful tone. 'We can't manage a party, love, but I'll try to bake a little cake. I've still got some marg and things left over from last week.'

'Thanks, Mum,' Deborah said, and kissed her in a sudden rush of affection and guilt at the lie she was about to tell. 'I'll be late home on Monday. There's a netball match after school.'

'Well, we'll cut the cake when your father comes home,' Pamela Jenkins said. 'Sixteen is too old for parties, but we'll have a little celebration.'

On the following Monday, Deborah woke up and remembered. She was sixteen today, she was meeting Warren today, and she had lied again to her parents. She was filled with apprehension, with a thrilling sensation of something momentous about to happen, and with happiness too. And the sun was shining!

'Happy birthday, darling,' her mother said at breakfast. Her father looked up from the newspaper which he was about to open and nodded. 'Sixteen!' he said. 'Well, enjoy yourself, and be good.'

'Right ho, Dad,' she said, fingers crossed again. She hoped neither of her parents would notice the colour that she could feel flaming in her face.

'Mum's made us cake,' she told him. 'We're to have it tonight, when you come home.'

'Good,' was all he said before opening the paper.

They met on the way home from

school, on the Durdham Downs. It was only a small detour. She hated the thought of Warren seeing her in school uniform, but there was nothing to be done about that. She dare not even remove her dreadful straw hat with its tell-tale red band. Summer term meant that black velour had changed to corn coloured straw. But pleasant red and white checked cotton dresses had replaced the ghastly gymslip and that was a bonus. She pulled her belt more tightly to emphasise her slim waist and stuffed her satchel into the saddlebag of the bike.

She saw him before he spotted her. They had arranged to meet at The White Tree, a local landmark. She watched him cycling along the road towards her and her heart filled with love and misery, both. Then suddenly he saw her, wobbled on the old bicycle, braked and skidded to a halt.

'Hi there, honey,' he said. 'It's just swell to see you again. I reckoned that when you didn't turn up on Saturdays you were through with me.'

'But you heard, didn't you? That it wasn't my fault, Warren? I'm forbidden to see you any more.'

'Got the message last Saturday. Not a word before then.'

She looked at him with desperation. What must he have thought? Had he found another girl? Her anger with her father bubbled up helplessly. 'My dad was furious,' she said. 'Stella's dad too. There was no way to get word to you. I'm so sorry, Warren.'

He looked at her, concerned, and pushed his bike nearer to hers. 'Don't think about it, honey,' he said. 'You're here now. That's all that matters.'

A small boy walking along the pavement was watching them. He stared at the American. 'Got any gum, mister?'

Warren grinned, propped his machine against the tree trunk and fished in his pockets. 'Sure, kid. Catch.' He threw a packet of chewing gum and a couple of Hershey bars in the child's direction.

The little boy scrabbled on the grass and ran off clutching his treasures. Then he turned to Deborah. 'I got something for you as well, honey. More chocolate, two bars. I guessed one of them might sweeten your mom and pop a bit.'

'I can't give it to them,' Deborah said. 'They'd kill me if they knew I'd seen you again.'

He looked mystified. 'What is it with these parents? What's wrong with us guys?'

She smiled, a small sad smile and shook her head. 'Nothing, Warren. Nothing at all.' She wanted to add, And I love you more than anything else in the world.

'Anyways,' he said, 'You're here now sweetheart. Best make the most of it.' He grinned at her. 'Let's go find some place. Anywhere private hereabouts?'

She nodded. 'Follow me, but keep your distance. If I'm seen I'll be expelled. I'm supposed to be playing netball.'

She cycled ahead of him for some time along the quiet road towards some deep hollows in the ground. As a child she had played here often. They were known as the Dumps, probably relics of some ancient workings, but now they were private secret places.

Warren looked around appreciatively. 'Gee, this is great.' He pushed both their bicycles under branches heavy with new spring leaf, then took off his jacket and spread it on the grass. 'Now, honey, what gives?'

She sat down sedately beside him. What gives, he said. Well what did 'give'? Just about everything! All the things she wanted to say to him were sealed up tightly in her heart like a coiled spring. How could she tell him that she loved him, how to say those magic words now, when she suspected that she might be having a baby, his baby, that she would be thrown out of home and out of school because of him. That she had nowhere to go and no-one to help her, and he was going off to war soon, leaving her to manage as best she could.

It was all too dreadful to think about. She had never been late before with the curse, regular as clockwork, no trouble. She had been thankful for that, but now it was a threat, a horrible threat to everything she knew, to her whole life. She wanted to die. Why did girls call it the curse? The blessing would be a more apt name.

She sniffed, pulled out her handkerchief and wiped her eyes and her nose, and then his arms were around her and she was crying into the soft fabric of his shirt.

'Hey there, what's the problem? Here I was real glad to see you after all those times you didn't show up at the dances, and now you cry all over me.'

Deborah tried to pull herself together. She had resolved not to tell him anything about her fears and she wasn't going to be diverted from that. He had a battle to face, and if it was different from hers, well that had to be.

They both had battles, and they would come through, and she would do nothing to worry him, to make his chances of survival any poorer.

If you were worried when you were facing an enemy you might not be thinking too clearly. They'd talked about that in history lessons. In war you had to be strong and resourceful. Women as well as men.

'Give me a cigarette,' she whispered. 'I'm OK really I am, just a bit sad that we can't meet any more except like this.'

He lit the cigarette for her, put it into her trembling fingers and she puffed inexpertly. She couldn't blow smoke into the air glamorously like they did at the pictures, and she'd never improve now because this was probably the last time in her life she'd smoke a cigarette. She wouldn't want to. It would remind her too much of Warren.

Tears gathered and she could see him looking at her with concern in his blue eyes. She made another supreme effort to hide her distress. 'You'll be going off to war soon won't you. I might never see you again.'

He grinned. 'Mustn't talk about that. Secret stuff. I don't know anything anyway. They keep us guys in the dark about plans. It's only the top brass gets to know when and where. Gee honey, you're sure beautiful in spite of that crazy gear you're wearing.'

He stubbed out his cigarette on the tree trunk behind them, took hers from her and did the same, then he kissed her. She could feel him breathing fast, and unwillingly she pushed him away. 'Not now, Warren,' she gasped. For some reason that she couldn't understand she suddenly didn't want him right now.

Was it because of the baby? Why was she feeling so contrary? She jumped to her feet, brushed bits of leaf and twig from her red blazer, grabbed her panama where it was swinging on the handlebars of her bike, and squashed it back on her head. Not caring now how she looked, she even put the elastic under her chin and then she pulled her bike from the bushes.

'This is goodbye,' she said. 'Sorry, Warren, but it really has to be for both our sakes.'

He looked quite smitten. 'Oh come on, Sweetheart, what's gotten into you? Why arrange this meeting if that's how you feel?' He was on his feet looking at her. He had never called her *Sweetheart* before today. Did it mean anything special? It was something she would remember for ever.

'When the war is over,' she said knowing that she was dreaming of some blissful time in a never-never-wonderland. 'When the war is over, if you haven't forgotten all about me, you can come back to England and look me up. We'll to go London. I've always wanted to go there.'

She wheeled her bicycle up the slope to the path above. Why had she said that she wondered? Why London? Because it was glamorous and exciting and she'd always thought that you could do what you liked in London. Not now of course with all the bombs, but one day, one wonderful day in that golden future she sometimes dreamed about. But now her voice was full of worry. 'Don't follow me, Warren. Please don't follow me. Someone might see us.'

'OK,' she heard him say. 'If that's how you want it, but I'll come back for you Deborah-honey. That's a right pretty name to stick in a guy's head. I'll come back and get you and carry you right off home when this damn war's over.' He didn't follow her though, and she suddenly felt that he didn't mean a word of it. She was probably just one of his conquests, a too-easy English girl convenient for filling in the time while he waited for his fate across the sea.

He let her get away on her own and although part of her wanted him to rush over the grass, to pull her off her bike and hold her, in spite of all her muddled and troubled thoughts, she peddled swiftly away along the path and on to the road towards home and the horrors that she knew awaited her in the future lonely weeks.

She saw the forgotten bars of chocolate five minutes later in her bicycle basket and her stomach heaved. Forbidden fruit! American riches signifying many things. She braked and stood with one foot on the pavement and wondered what she could do with them. Two boys were running along towards her and she called to them.

'Want some chocolate?'

They stopped frozen in their tracks. 'That's Yankee chocolate,' one of them said staring into her bicycle basket. 'You been with them Yanks, then?' He held out his hand. 'I like Yanks. I like 'em lots.'

'I like them too,' she said and she felt the tears again hot behind her eyes. This time she let them flow.

3

'They've gone!' Deborah, clasping her school books close to her chest like a shield, was near to tears one day at school a couple of weeks later.

'Who's gone, what are you talking about?' Maureen stared at her friend.

'The Americans of course. Surely you must have seen all the trucks and tanks and things heading out of town?' Deborah groped for her handkerchief, sniffed, dabbed at her eyes, and nearly dropped her books. 'We shall never see them again.'

'I thought you didn't want to anyway.' Maureen shrugged and her voice was unsympathetic.

'That was then,' Deborah sniffed. 'Now that it's happened it's quite different. I suppose I didn't really believe that he could just . . . ' She groped for words. 'Vanish as though he'd never been.'

The girls were on their way from one school building to the other. To French, and a gruelling lesson with their enthusiastic French teacher who had, earlier in the war, made them stand and sing *La Marseillaise* regularly once a week. Lately, as signs of the invasion gathered momentum she had become almost ecstatic.

As soon as the class had filed into the room she beamed at them. 'Today we must work hard,' she said. 'Soon my country will be free again, and you will go to France. You will see its beauty. You will visit Paris.' She made it sound like paradise.

Deborah thought that London would do quite well. London would certainly do if only she had Warren at her side. She stared at her teacher hardly hearing the words but registering the excitement. 'So you must do well with your French, mes enfants.'

Yes, she must work hard for there was little else to do just now. Yet through the jubilant words Deborah saw, through a blur of tears, and in her imagination, the mangled body of Warren and thousands of others who would soon be fighting to bring this glorious victory about. She put up her hand.

'Yes, Deborah?'

'How long do you think it will be, Mademoiselle, before our forces land in France, and how long before they liberate Paris?'

'I have no idea. The sooner the better of course.' She put her fingers to her lips. 'But we must not talk about it or try to guess. The walls have ears, children. We must just pray that it's soon.'

Deborah looked out of the window and then back to her teacher and the classroom. A whole mass of soldiers from many different allied countries, fighting together for freedom from Hitler, made it all sound wonderfully heroic, but when you knew and loved one of them, two in fact because Luke was still in the thick of it somewhere, then it became frightening and horrible. 'Do you think many will be killed?' she said, and her voice held such passion that some of her classmates stared at her with amazement.

Her teacher was obviously taken aback. 'C'est inevitable,' she said. 'They are all very brave young men.' She put on her half glasses and peered at Deborah over the top of them, then opened a book on the desk before her. 'But we must all work for this brave new world they are fighting for.' She suddenly became brisk and efficient. 'Please now turn to page twenty and we will read together, and then translate.'

Deborah stared at the page before her, and imagined the beaches, the gunfire, the bombs. She'd seen enough of bombs in Bristol earlier in the war and Maureen had told her something of the ruins in London. Maureen's grandmother lived in a place called Chiswick. She ran a Salvation Army hostel and wouldn't give up her good work to go to the country away from the bombs.

'She takes in 'fallen girls',' Maureen had said. 'But it's a nice place. We used to stay there when we visited. Everyone seemed happy in spite of being fallen!'

Deborah remembered giggling with her friend about the words. They hadn't known then just what 'fallen' meant and had guessed at all sorts of fantastic things.

Now, with a little more knowledge, the word held an amount of fear and apprehension. How in the world could any girl allow herself to get into this dire situation?

Again there had been many more guesses, but now that Deborah had discovered the truth, she realised that it was more terrible than either of them had imagined. Should she consider herself 'fallen'? It was a frightening thought. Not funny any more.

That evening Deborah threw off her school clothes and stood naked in front of the long mirror in her bedroom. She turned sideways, looked dispassionately at her slim body and wondered how long it would take to show. She'd missed two curses now and when she thought of the child growing relentlessly inside her she was both frantic with worry and at the same time strangely elated.

Warren's child! When he lay dead on some French beach or field she would have a permanent memory of him, some part of him that would live on. Perhaps it was worth the horrors and the shame. It made her feel that she had some small part to play in the war and the battle that was to come however unimaginably hard it all would be.

But what if he survived? Would he come looking for her? Could she hope for such a double miracle? She threw on a dull brown summer dress that her mother had made from some material bought at a salvage sale and pulled the belt tightly around her waist. The dress wasn't a tight fit and that was a good thing she thought dully. Hopefully it would do for a good few weeks yet.

During that summer Deborah sat her

School Certificate examination. With steely determination she tried to put all thoughts of the future aside, and to her own amazement was sure that she had done well.

But her father would not let anyone forget the war. Every morning at breakfast he read the latest newspaper headlines aloud, and when at last, in June, the great day arrived, D Day, the day of salvation for the world, as he called it, Deborah tried not to hear his jubilant voice. And each morning after that he proclaimed one victory after another. He announced these small advances with as much pride as if he himself was responsible.

Soon after the landings he read, 'Allied Supreme Headquarters have stated that progress has continued along the whole of the Normandy beachhead,' and a few days later he was even more ecstatic as he rustled the front page triumphantly. 'American troops move inland after heavy fighting on beaches.' He pointed to a large photograph. 'Look at this. We've got Jerry on the run at last.'

Deborah nearly choked on her cornflakes and refused to look at the photograph, imagining Warren lying there on the Normandy shore.

By the time the exam results came through and she learnt that she had passed with three distinctions and four credits, the allied invasion was proclaimed a success, the Germans were in slow retreat, the end of the war was in sight. Not for a long time, but certainly in sight. The country was jubilant, but Deborah was becoming increasingly frantic.

'You'll have to tell your father soon,' her mother announced one morning during the August holidays.

Deborah stared at her. 'What?' She felt giddy with shock.

'I've known for a long time. Look at you, no waist visible, and it isn't what you eat. You'll have to tell him today when he comes home. You won't be able to go back to school in September of course. It was one of those Yanks I suppose.'

Deborah nodded bleakly. Her mother was so matter-of-fact, so composed. 'How long have you known?' she said. 'Why didn't you say?'

'Long enough.' Her mother sat down on the hard upright chair that stood in front of her sewing machine. 'I didn't say anything because there was nothing I could bring myself to say. You've broken my heart, Deborah.' She shook her head, her composure breaking down now. 'I was always glad that you were a girl and wouldn't have to join up, but this is worse. At least if you'd been a son we might have been proud to see you in uniform.'

She groped in her apron pocket for a handkerchief and dabbed at her eyes. 'Now all you've done is bring us shame and disgrace. Your father will send you away. You know that don't you?'

Deborah nodded. She went to her mother and put her arms around her.

'Oh, Mummy, I'm so sorry, so very very sorry.'

'Sorry isn't much good. You've thrown your life away, that's what you've done, and all for a bit of wayward pleasure.' She sniffed and blew her nose. But then she held her daughter close and smoothed her unruly hair. 'I still love you, Deborah, and as long I live I'll always help you. But I can't gainsay your father. If he says you've got to go, as he will, then there's nothing I can do.'

'Will you tell him for me?' Deborah stared out of the window at the back yard and small patch of garden. What was going to happen to her? What about the neighbours? What would happen to her parents? She was their only child. There were no brothers or sisters to soften the blow. How would they live with the disgrace?

Her mother shook her head. 'It's your job to tell him.'

'Please, please do it for me,' Deborah pleaded. 'I couldn't face him. I wouldn't know what to say. I absolutely couldn't do it.'

Pamela Jenkins considered her daughter, thought for a moment of her own youth. Perhaps after all she might be able to sweeten him up a bit first. A sudden smile spread over her face and was as quickly erased.

There had been that night years back when Brian asked her to marry him. He'd done the proper thing, asked her father first, but then they'd walked on the Downs, the very place where Deborah had probably gone with her American, and of course what followed there under the stars had been just the same.

She remembered the fear afterwards, the day before she was reassured that nothing frightful was going to follow, and the blessed relief of that longed for period. Deborah had not been so lucky. Life was hard for women, she thought, hard of course for men too during this war, but really tough on womenfolk in different ways. Men going off to fight and probably die, expected everything.

She nodded thoughtfully. 'All right then. I'll tell him. After tea it'll be. When he's settled with his pipe and slippers, then I'll break the news. You go up to your bedroom — make some excuse. I'll do my best to soften the blow.' She got up and started to clear the breakfast things from the table.

Deborah threw her arms around her all over again nearly knocking the teapot from her hand. 'Thank you, oh thank you, Mummy, a thousand thousand times,' she said. 'You're wonderful. Do you really think Dad will throw me out? I can't bear it.'

'Well you'll have to won't you. I'll suggest that Sarah might take you in until it's all over. Perhaps he'll let you go there if he's in any state to listen.'

Aunt Sarah! Luke and Simon's mum. Deborah thought of her with sudden relief. She had always loved Aunt Sarah. The holidays she had spent there at Exmouth before the war had been wonderful. The house had always been full of fun and happiness. 'Oh, Mum, that would be wonderful. Do you think he'll agree?'

'That's as maybe. Perhaps he will, perhaps he won't. And your aunt might not be too keen either. She's changed since she heard that Simon was a prisoner of the Japanese, and she's always worried about Luke fighting somewhere. She's not the cheerful soul she used to be.'

'Perhaps she'd like some company,' Deborah said. 'I could try to cheer her up a bit.'

'In your state?'

'I'd try.'

'You'd have to get a wedding ring, pretend you were married.'

Deborah left the comfort of her mother's arms and slumped down at the breakfast table. She put her head in her hands. 'I suppose I would,' she mumbled. 'But I'd hate it, Mum, all the lies and that.' She thought of the brass curtain rings from Woolworth's which she'd heard some girls were wearing. It would be, for her, a mark of shame instead of happiness and triumph.

'You can have your grandmother's ring,' her mother said, reading her thoughts. 'She'd be turning in her grave if she knew what you'd done, but she was kind and I know she'd want to help, so you can have it.'

Deborah turned stricken eyes upon her mother and then she stood up, took the old grimed kettle from the hob and carried it into the scullery, poured the water into the chipped enamel bowl with a handful of soda, and started to wash up.

She waited in fearful anxiety all that day and after tea she escaped to her bedroom. She left the door ajar and she could hear her parents talking, knew that her mother was breaking the news as gently as she could, was trying to calm her father. Then she heard his voice gradually rising to a crescendo, heard him stop stomping through the passage into the parlour, and eventually the summons came.

'Deborah, come down here at once. Into the front room.'

She crept down the stairs holding the banister rail for support. The front room of the house, the parlour, was only used for special guests or momentous events. He was standing in front of the empty fireplace. She could feel his eyes upon her, staring at her stomach and she flinched and pulled herself in as flat as she could.

'Your mother tells me that you are expecting. I need to hear it from your lips, Deborah. Is this true?'

She nodded. 'Yes.' The one word was all she could manage.

'And who is responsible? One of the Yanks that I have forbidden you to see, I suppose?'

This time she could only nod again helplessly.

Her father took a deep breath. 'Then I cannot insist you marry him. He's probably stitched up in a body bag somewhere in France by now.'

The words were cruel, but Deborah

had recently changed her mind about facing the awful facts. Reluctantly she had read the newspaper reports for herself and had agonised over photographs and numbers of soldiers killed. She would never see Warren again. Of that she was quite sure. She dabbed at her eyes.

'You'll have to get rid of it.'

Deborah gasped. This was an option she had not really considered. It was against the law, usually highly dangerous. 'Dad,' she said. 'You don't really mean that I should find some . . . ' She couldn't finish.

He shook his head impatiently. 'No, of course I don't mean that. You're my daughter, my only child, and in spite of this folly you have committed I wouldn't want you to break the law or be in danger. You'll have it adopted as soon as it's born.'

He took a deep breath and slowly took his pipe from his pocket, pressed on the tobacco absentmindedly, then fumbled to light it. Deborah hoped that he might mellow a little with the comfort of an intake of tobacco, but it was not to be.

'And now, you will leave this house within the week. I don't want to see you again until the child is born and taken away. I've loved you very much all your life, and I can't bear to see your disgrace. When it's all over you can come home.'

She looked up at him, unbelieving. 'I have to go away? Immediately?' It was more than she could bear at this moment. 'Where am I to go?'

He shrugged his shoulder. 'There are various establishments around the country I believe. They take in girls of fallen and despicable natures, I am told.'

'And you would really send me to one of those?'

'Undoubtedly.' He looked at her coldly. 'Your mother tells me that your aunt might take you, and I suppose that would be preferable. But if not we shall have to make other arrangements.'

Unexpectedly his tone softened a little. 'You've ruined your life, Deborah. I hope you realise that, and you've destroyed your mother and me with your wickedness.'

He turned his back on her and she could see the shaking of his shoulders and knew that he was crying. She had never seen a man cry before, didn't even know that they could. She wanted to cross the room to him, throw her arms around him as she had done to her mother, but there was a great gulf between them now, and however much she wished to bridge it, she was incapable of doing so. She felt her heart would break for misery.

4

A few days later a letter arrived from Aunt Sarah. Yes, she could go there until the baby was born. It was lonely with the boys away and she had always wanted a daughter, she wrote. She would be glad of the company.

And so, the following day, with battered suitcase packed, Deborah and her mother caught the bus to Temple Meads Station and stood with soldiers, sailors, airmen and a few civilians like themselves. Deborah looked around at the throng and felt suddenly all alone, alone to face whatever horrors waited for her. She knew that she had brought it all on herself, and this made it much worse.

She wished now that she had been a boy, perhaps one of the group of jolly young sailors going presumably to a ship at Plymouth. They looked as though they hadn't a care in the world. At least her parents wouldn't have been ashamed. Scared for their child's safety, yes, but not humiliated as they now believed themselves to be.

She forced herself to think of the other people on the crowded platform. There were two RAF pilots. She could see the wings proudly displayed on their uniforms, and a sprinkling of girls in Wren uniforms stood close by. How she envied them.

Soon the train south to Exeter and Plymouth would arrive, both destinations nearer to the scenes of action, nearer to the fighting and action, and perhaps glorious victory. They would all be carried away to their fates, their adventures, or perhaps their deaths. Yet they all seemed brimming with confidence and good spirits.

Deborah tried to be optimistic too. After all it was better to think of surviving this war, or this trouble, or whatever life threw at you, than to give in and think you were just going to die.

That way would give in to Hitler. Mr Churchill was an optimist. Deborah thought of him now and his great speeches that had kept them all going when things were really tough. She smiled at her mother.

The two women stood silently not knowing what to say to each other at this fraught time in each of their lives. At last Deborah plucked up the courage to ask the question that haunted her of late. 'What's it like, Mum? Having a baby?'

Pamela Jenkins drew in her breath ominously. 'You'll get through it,' she said. 'You're young and strong. Of course, if there's a baby that you're wanting at the end of it, then it's worthwhile.'

It wasn't the answer she wanted to hear. A baby that you're wanting! Deborah thought about the words and wondered if perhaps she did want this baby after all? No, of course she didn't. But sometimes she had to admit to a feeling of sympathy for the poor little thing. How awful if that sentiment should turn into love!

The train eventually steamed noisily into the station and came to a shuddering halt, thus stopping further disturbing thoughts and all conversation.

'Bye, Mummy,' Deborah said. She hugged her mother close for a few seconds and then picked up her case and pushed her way to the front of the platform and into the carriage. There were no seats, but she managed to find a place in the corridor next to the door and the open window.

She waved disconsolately to the brave and quickly vanishing little figure of her mother as the train pulled away and rounded the bend in the line, and then she sat on her suitcase and thought a trifle glumly about her future.

Aunt Sarah was round and homely looking. She had brought a little wooden handcart to the station to take Deborah's luggage. 'Hope you don't mind this contraption,' she said after they had kissed and hugged each other. 'It's better than carrying it all the way.'

Deborah grinned. 'I remember it, Aunt Sarah. Luke used to push me in it when we were little.' They lumped the suitcase into it and each took one of the handles, and then they laughed at all the humps and bumps in the road all the way home. When at last they reached the little house by the sea, Deborah began to think that perhaps life might not be so empty and forlorn as she had thought. Her positive thoughts were beginning to reassert themselves again.

'You can have Luke's room,' her aunt told her as she unlocked the front door. 'He won't be needing it for a few months yet.'

Deborah remembered the house, the smell and sound of the sea that was all part of it and that had always filled her with excitement when she was a little girl. It meant holidays, sand castles, Mummy and Daddy sitting on the beach in deckchairs, and sometimes an ice-cream. Jelly for tea with Devon clotted cream, and her two cousins, Luke and Simon charging over the sand kicking a football and sometimes dragging her into the waves, laughing, dunking her under, and then pulling her out and racing her back to Mummy who was always ready with a big towel and a hug.

The years seemed to go backwards as she thought about those days. And now they were both in the forces. She wondered if she would ever see them again.

She wouldn't dwell on the gloomy things, but think only of the happy ones. 'Thank you so much for having me,' she said to her aunt. 'I've always loved it here. We used to have such fun.'

Aunt Sarah smiled at her. 'And we'll have fun again,' she said, with what seemed like forced brightness, 'when the boys come home. Now, come upstairs and leave your things, and then we'll have a nice cup of tea. I've made us a cake to celebrate.'

Deborah followed her up the creaking staircase. Celebrate what, she wondered as she looked around the room? The boys had always shared this bedroom when she and her parents came to stay for the one wonderful week's holiday every summer. Now it was hers until the baby was born, until she could go back home to Bristol, to school again perhaps, or more likely to a job.

'It's a nice little room,' her aunt said. 'I gave it a special spring-clean for you, and I cleared out some of Luke's things.' She opened the wardrobe door and revealed a few empty wooden hangers. 'There you are, love.'

Deborah saw her aunt brush her hand across her eyes and knew that all this handling of Luke's clothes had taken some courage. She hugged her gratefully. 'He'll be home safe and sound,' she said, hardly daring to believe it. 'You'll see.'

'Of course he will.'

Aunt Sarah left the wardrobe door

open and bustled out of the room. 'I'll put the kettle on.'

Deborah took off her cardigan and put it on the bed, and then she opened her suitcase and put her few clothes in the cupboard with Luke's shirts and his one good suit. She touched them reverently, and remembered how once, when she was just beginning to change from child to teenager she had thought herself in love with him.

That was towards the beginning of the war when she was about twelve years old. She could remember fantasising about him during those holidays as she lay on the little camp bed in her parents' room in this house all those years ago. Then he had been called up and she had only seen him briefly when he was on leave.

He'd visited her family in Bristol a couple of times but it all seemed a long time ago. Simon, fighting in the Far East, and now a prisoner, had not been home for a long time. Her aunt worried about them constantly.

Until she met Warren, both cousins had been in Deborah's thoughts frequently. Luke had written to her occasionally, short notes that she had treasured and kept in the little lock-up box beside her bed at home along with the photograph taken on the beach one happy carefree holiday afternoon. It showed a tall boy with a mop of dark curly hair and a funny knitted bathing costume. He was laughing and he held a rubber beach ball in his hands. She remembered that he had thrown it at her soon afterwards.

Now, in his room and surrounded by his things, she had the strangest feeling that he was with her somehow. Would he condemn? Certainly he would be sad for her predicament. She looked at his photograph splendid in his uniform, and at his cricket bat hanging beside it on the wall, proudly displayed. She felt she had let him down horribly, had let her whole family down.

'Tea's made,' her aunt called up the stairs and Deborah left her suitcase open on the bed with its few remaining bits and pieces still unpacked, and she ran down to the front parlour where there was a trolley laid carefully with the best china. A bobbly tea-cosy over the pot, and a cake on a glass stand.

'To celebrate,' Aunt Sarah said again.

'I didn't think my coming like this was worthy of a celebration,' Deborah said. 'Dad wouldn't have thought so anyway.'

'Fiddlesticks. I'm really glad to have you, dear. And we have to be grateful that the war's going well. The boys will soon be home and it'll be all over.'

There it was again, the brave optimism and Deborah could have wept for all the mums and dads and wives who kept on saying things like this. But it was good, the right thing to say. Yet she suddenly felt weepy again. She wished the tears wouldn't come totally unbidden and so frequently.

She glanced at the newspaper lying on the sofa before she sat down. *Allies drive Germans from Normandy*, the headlines now joyfully proclaimed. She should be rejoicing like Aunt Sarah instead of feeling so gloomy, on the surface anyway. It was important to keep smiling even if your heart was breaking inside.

Her aunt cut two large slices from the cake, put one piece on a plate and handed it to Deborah. 'There, dear. Eat it all up. I saved the rations for three weeks to make this. You've got to eat for two now you know.'

Deborah took the plate. 'Thank you. It looks delicious.' She ate some and smiled. It was very good. Her mother had not made cakes like this for a long time. She was touched that her aunt had done this for her. Perhaps here in the safety of this comfortable little home she could talk about the coming baby, speak of her fears and of her growing misery at having to give it up.

These unwanted feelings had been increasing ever since she had felt the child move within her. It had become a dependent tiny living thing rather than 'the result of sin' as her father declared. She felt protective of this unborn scrap, and those feelings made the future unbearably bleak.

'I'm so grateful, Aunt Sarah, that you don't mind having me,' she said. 'I couldn't have stayed at home. Daddy was very angry. He relented a bit later on, but he was still too ashamed to have me around.'

'Your father is a good man, but a child of his time and his religion,' Sarah said. 'I knew him before he married your mother and I was dismayed at first when she told me that she was going to marry him. But he's mellowed over the years. The young are often very forthright and determined and as a young man he would have been even more scandalised. He had his moments too though.'

Deborah looked at her in surprise. 'What do you mean, Aunt?'

Sarah laughed. 'In the same place as you fell for your American I expect. In those enticing old hollows on the

Downs. Your mother and I were good friends and we shared all our secrets. She came to my house with a glowing face one evening and told me what had happened. Then of course there were two weeks of agonising worry before she knew that she had been lucky and there would be no unfortunate consequences of that one foolish moment.'

Deborah blushed. Her aunt was talking to her as though she were quite grown up. She was talking about things that you just didn't discuss, that made you horribly embarrassed. But she was completely stunned too by what her aunt had told her. 'You don't mean that Mummy and Daddy . . . ' She couldn't finish the sentence.

'Many people who think they are perfection itself have feet of clay. It's the human condition, my dear, so don't worry over much about your father's reaction. He'll come round.'

'He won't let me keep the baby though.'

Aunt Sarah nodded. 'Well that's

probably all for the good,' she said. 'You want to get a job and a new life, marry one day perhaps. Then there'll be other babies and you'll forget this one.'

Deborah stared at her. So even lovely warm Aunt Sarah drew the line at keeping illegitimate babies. That would be absolutely beyond the pale. She didn't really want to finish the piece of cake on her plate now, but she forced herself to eat some more.

'Perhaps you're right,' she said, not believing a word of it. She put her hand on her stomach and tried to send a message to the tiny thing growing there. 'I'll always love you,' she said silently in her head. 'I'll always love you whatever they make me do with you.'

Every day when Deborah read the newspaper she became increasingly resentful of the war. She felt that it had ruined her life, everyone's life of course, but when in late August she said something of this she was surprised by her aunt's response.

'You don't know what you're talking about, my girl. No-one forced you to go out with your American did they?' She took the newspaper from the table and pointed to an article on the front page. 'Look at this for a moment and then tell me that the war has ruined your life!'

Deborah took the paper and read again the report of a concentration camp just liberated at a place called Maidanek where hundreds of innocent people had been slaughtered, gassed apparently. She breathed deeply and didn't know how to reply.

'And what about the flying bombs falling on London, the doodle-bugs that are killing so many just when we thought the war was nearly won and we'd seen the last of all that?' Aunt Sarah got up from the breakfast table and began gathering dishes on to a tray. 'And our forces fighting just about everywhere it seems.'

Deborah knew that she was thinking of Luke and Simon. 'I'm sorry, Aunt

Sarah,' she whispered. 'Down here in Devon it's easy to forget all the horrors and to think only of myself and what's to become of me.' She wanted to add, and my baby too, but didn't dare. That would be just too thoughtless.

'Paris is free now though,' she said. It was the one piece of news during the month which had made any sense to her, which had lodged in her mind and which made her remember her school and Mademoiselle's lessons. The little French woman would have been rejoicing on that day.

Aunt Sarah nodded. 'Well, I suppose we needed a bit of something to cheer us up,' she said. She cleared away the rest of the stuff from their breakfast and took the cloth carefully and shook the crumbs out of back door then folded it and put it in the drawer beneath the table.

Deborah just sat there and watched her, and wondered how the war would be going by the time her baby was born, just four months away now. It would be a Christmas or New Year child.

She found it very difficult sometimes to think of the future. Warren seemed a whole world away, if indeed he had survived that first frightful assault on Normandy's beaches, and even if he had, then she was pretty sure he wouldn't come looking for her after the war. She felt, more and more lately, that she had just been a small side-line in his life, something to take his mind off the uncertainty, the fear of the battle to come, for surely there must have been fear. Men liked war though, appeared to be made for it, but they knew it wasn't all glory and excitement didn't they?

'You wash the dishes and clear up, and I'll go and see what the butcher can offer us for our dinner,' Aunt Sarah said, bringing Deborah back from her dreary thoughts.

She jumped up guiltily and went to her aunt and hugged her. Displays of affection had not often taken place at home, but here it was different. 'Forgive me for being a selfish pig?' she said.

'Of course,' Sarah said. 'We're all selfish at heart.'

Deborah felt even more selfish and considerably worried too when the telegram came at the end of October. Luke had been badly wounded in the furious battle for Corfu and was in a military hospital somewhere in England.

'How badly wounded?' Aunt Sarah wondered aloud. Her face had gone almost as white as the tablecloth on which she had dropped the telegram as though it was some poisonous viper. 'It doesn't say.' She picked it up again and read it again, then stared at it with unbelieving eyes. 'I must go to him,' she said. 'I must find out where he is and go at once.'

She looked at Deborah, distracted and fraught. 'You'll have to go back to Bristol, love. I can't leave you here alone.'

Deborah was immediately terrified.

She shook her head. 'Dad would never let me go home. I'll be all right, Aunt Sarah. You go. Please, please let me stay here. I'll look after the house while you're away and make everything nice and welcoming for when Luke comes home.'

Sarah frowned distractedly. 'If it wasn't for the baby it might be all right, but even then I'd be worried. I'll write to your father tonight.'

5

In spite of all Deborah's tears, the letter was sent and the reply received. Her father had made arrangements for her to go to a hostel in Weston-Super-Mare. She could stay there until the baby was born, then it would be taken by the Welfare for adoption and she could come home.

Deborah stared at his letter with anger and frustration. Even now in this emergency her parents were failing her. To everyone the baby was an embarrassment and an inconvenience, something to be forgotten and erased as though the whole event had never happened. She cradled her stomach in her arms and lay awake tearful for a long time.

'It's a place for girls in a delicate situation,' Aunt Sarah said the next morning trying to soften the blow when

Deborah appeared red-eyed at breakfast.

'You mean fallen girls, don't you?' Deborah thought of her school friend, Maureen, and the home her grandmother ran in London. Maureen had always said how pleasant it was. And it was then, that the beginnings of an alternative plan began to worm its way into her mind.

'It's only until I can get Luke home,' Aunt Sarah said. 'Then you can come back here and we'll look after him together.'

But Deborah was horrified at this idea too. Luke just mustn't see her in this hugely pregnant state. She'd die of shame especially when she had to tell him that it was a GI who was the father. This thought gave even more impetus to her rather scary idea.

The next night she refused to weep, but lay in bed and planned her escape from all those who were dictating her life for her. She'd write a letter to the place in Weston and sign it in her mother's name saying that she wouldn't be going there after all. Then she would change her railway ticket for one to London.

She would just disappear until the baby was born. That way she would be free to make her own decisions. No-one could tell her what to do about the baby, and if she wanted to keep it, well then, in London she would be free to do so. She could get a job, manage somehow. She refused to think of the difficulties, refused to let her common sense take over, and for the first time in many weeks she began to know a strange sense of happiness. Her parents' rejection made her feel hard and determined. She would do just as she pleased for once.

Chiswick was where Maureen's grand-mother ran this home for people, girls mostly, who needed help. In spite of her new independence, Deborah knew very well that she needed help, but she wanted it on her terms. Maureen had always stayed there on family visits and she said how decent it was, and how kind her grandmother was. It was a happy place. To Deborah at this time it appeared a sort of haven. And London was exciting, anonymous. She could give a false name and no-one would be able to trace her.

Quite suddenly the future seemed to hold some promise instead of being totally black. She would be in charge of her life. She had thirty pounds saved. It was in her post office savings book under the mattress. She'd brought it with her to Exmouth and now she put her hand down and felt its reassuring presence. Somehow she would scheme and plan, and get to London and freedom. But of course, she knew that she would write to her mother.

Tears came to eyes when she thought of Pamela Jenkins, a small slight figure always submissive to her father, never having her own way about anything. It would be a letter explaining everything except where she was. She would tell her how she felt about the baby, about wanting to decide for herself what to do about it. She would talk about freedom and choice.

Of course her mother wouldn't understand, but then you never knew. Deborah hoped that at least their love for each other might survive this frightful thing she intended to do.

Deborah never quite knew how she eventually reached London. The nightmare journey became a blur in her mind, blotted out by what happened afterwards. She remembered that people had been kind to her, soldiers mostly, and that she had lied repeatedly, saying that her husband had been killed on the Normandy beaches and she was going to his mother in Chiswick.

She wanted her baby to be born there she had said, in his home. Indeed she had repeated this story so many times, both in her head, and aloud, that she almost came to believe it herself. No Yankee father, no Warren, just some fictional English Tommy whom she had married on a forty-eight hour leave back in the spring.

But as she told her story another part of her mind was becoming doubtful about this place Maureen had talked about. They might probe, ask too many questions. Perhaps a room of her own might be more anonymous. She would get a bus to Chiswick anyway. The hostel could be a last resort.

Paddington was noisy, crowded and dirty, no wondrous magic here at all, and she stood there holding her one small suitcase. To her despair the excitement was giving way to doubt. She had no idea at all of what to do next. All her previous courage and determination had departed like the fickle autumn sun.

'Want some help, love?'

She looked at the porter and wondered how much she would have to give him if she accepted his offer. Sixpence? She couldn't afford to waste even sixpence so she shook her head. 'No thank you.'

'There might be some buses still running outside,' he said, nodding in the direction of the station exit. 'Where you going?'

'Chiswick,' she said without thinking. It was the only name she knew.

'Bloomin' lot of damage there,' he said. 'Pardon me, Ma'am, but them buzz bombs and rockets haven't made the place look very pretty.' He stared at her heavily rounded figure and she blushed. 'You best get yourself home as quick as you can.' He turned away to help an elderly woman with an enormous battered suitcase and Deborah felt herself sway on the platform as the uncaring crowds rushed past her in all directions.

Of course she had been silly to come here, absolutely crazy. What had possessed her? Now all she wanted to see was a friendly face, to be offered a cup of tea, and a bed for the night.

In a daze she walked to the exit and looked up and down the street outside and gasped at the damage. She'd seen whole streets of buildings smashed to rubble in Bristol, but that was two years ago. The night skies at home had been quieter for some months, and in Devon, if you didn't count the invasion exercises that her aunt had told her about, it was more peaceful still. But it was obviously very different here. What was it the man had said? Buzz bombs? Rockets? Yes, of course. She had discounted them, but now she was frightened.

Miraculously there was a bus and she nervously hailed it.

'Where to, darlin'?' The conductor held out his hand for her money.

'Chiswick.'

'Not sure if we'll get through,' he said, 'thanks to them bleedin' great V2s.' He punched a ticket for her and asked her for twopence.

'Will you tell me where to get off,' Deborah said. Then, a little common sense resurfacing in her brain, she added, 'I need to find a room. Can you tell me where to look?'

He stared at her and frowned. 'Well, there's a lot of cards advertise them things on the corner where I live. We pass it. I'll put you off there if you like.' He punched another ticket for a woman sitting next to her and then, before he went onto the man behind he paused and stared at her again. 'You don't sound like you belong round here. Where you come from?'

'Devon,' she said without thinking.

'Blimey, then you'd better get back there pretty damn quick. Especially in your condition. I'm blowed if I'd leave Devon for this hell-hole.' He turned away and went on down the swaying lurching bus and she watched him go with despair and panic.

She knew that he was absolutely right. She looked out of the window at the grisly ruins of houses and shops reduced to rubble, much of it still lying on the road.

'Bloomin' Jerries,' the woman next to her muttered. 'Thought the war was almost over, we did, and then they dump this lot on us.' She put her arms round the shopping bag on her lap and clutched it to her as though it was all she had left in the world. 'Lost my sister last week, her and all her family. All wiped out in one of them V2 rockets.' She dabbed her eyes with a dirty piece of cloth. 'My turn next shouldn't wonder.'

The bus swerved round potholes and uncleared debris and Deborah felt more and more sick. What on earth was she doing in this benighted place? She thought of getting off the bus and doing just as the conductor had said, going back to Paddington and taking the very next train to somewhere, anywhere but here. But then she was suddenly filled with protective love for her baby. She was doing this for him. She had to stay here and give birth to Warren's child.

Her made-up story vanished from her mind. She twirled her grandmother's ring on her finger. Warren! Her American, her Yank, her baby's dad. He was probably dead, so this baby was all that there was left in memory of him. Yes, she'd be strong and brave at least until she could see this child, cuddle him, and give him all the love that he deserved.

She closed her eyes, not wanting to see the horrors outside the window, seeing instead Bristol and the Durdham Downs, and Warren in his smart uniform putting his arms around her. Then she saw Luke in her mind. Sensible nice honest Luke. Oh Luke, what have I done? But she was suddenly brought back to the miserable present as the conductor pulled the bell and the bus lurched to a stop.

'There you are, darlin', there's the place I told you of. Plenty of rooms to rent advertised in the window.' He stood close to her and she could smell his sweat as he pointed to a seedy little post office on the other side of the road. 'No-one with any sense wants to stay in this place.'

In spite of his insensitive words, he gave her a hand with her luggage and helped her off the bus. 'Good luck!' he called, and she stood on the pavement amidst the dust and rubble and felt that this must be a terrible nightmare from which she would soon awake. She would find herself and her baby in some sun drenched never-never land, Warren or Luke at her side, someone to look after her and no cares in the world.

She crossed the road and stood looking at the newspaper stand and then at the row of cards in the dirty fly-blown window of the shop.

Careful gentlemen tenant they mostly said. *No children, five shillings per week.* She was just mentally trying to work out how long her money would last when an explosion tore suddenly through the street and she was thrown to the ground with a force she had never experienced in her life before.

Newspapers, debris, glass and stones were hurtling through the air all around her as the whole world seemed to crumble. The deafening blast spread like a great wave, lifting roofs and blowing fronts of buildings outwards to send them crashing into the street.

Screams mingled with the menacing sound of the blast and then a sturdy plank of wood came to rest on top of Deborah as she struggled to get to her feet. Its edges must have lodged on something because she found that she was trapped in a space, that its whole weight was not totally bearing down upon her. But she couldn't move.

More debris came reigning down, her mouth full of dust, and her screams mingled with all the other frantic cries for help that she could hear from all around. Then gradually the world became silent, and she was completely still, knowing nothing more.

After a long time, or a short time, for Deborah was aware of nothing at first, some voices began to penetrate her mind. Frantic shouting voices were calling to her, but she could make no sense of what they said. What had happened? Where was she?

Carefully, they dug her out, but as

they dug more rubble fell and she wandered in and out of consciousness. Then she felt herself being carried. She lay still on the stretcher and stared up at the grey sky and the smoke. Her lips formed some words, but she had no idea what she said.

She lay for the rest of that week in a bleak hospital ward, washed and comfortable, but still she had no idea who she was or why she was there. Nurses asked gentle questions, people came and went, and a doctor with a swinging stethoscope around his neck examined her, asked for her name, but she just stared up at him blankly with nothing in her mind at all, no means of communicating anything. She shook her head constantly, and every day her hands rested on the swell of her stomach. What was the matter with her? Tears came to her eyes as she tried to remember.

'You're going to have a baby, love,' a nurse said. 'You've got to get strong and tell us where your hubby is.'

She twisted her grandmother's ring on her finger and gradually a few dim memories came into her mind. Hubby? Of course, she was expecting, pretending to be married. The complications of it all filled her with dread. She closed her eyes and sank again into a deep semi-conscious sleep.

The next day she awoke suddenly full of fear. Someone was doing something under her bed. 'What happened to me?' she called. It was the first sensible thing she had said in the whole week.

The cleaner straightened up, dustpan and brush in hand. She looked at Deborah sympathetically. 'A buzz bomb, darlin'. You got caught by one of them silent devils, silent till they explode right over yer head. You was one of the lucky ones, just a few cuts and bruises I 'eard 'em say.'

Deborah stared at the woman uncomprehending. She still couldn't move very easily, but automatically groped for her bag. 'Bag?' she whispered. 'My things?'

The cleaner beckoned to a nurse.

'She seems to be comin' back to us,' she said.

The nurse breezed over and smiled. 'Hello, dear? Remembering things for us then?'

Deborah shook her head and then realised how much it hurt. She put her hand up and felt the bandage. 'What happened?' she whispered again.

'You hurt your head when the bomb exploded. You'll soon be fine.' The words were cheerful and confident.

'My bag?'

'Don't trouble about that now, dear. It might still turn up when all the rubble has been cleared. But you're safe and sound, that's the main thing. You just tell us your name and we'll be able to contact your family.'

Alarm bells began to ring in Deborah's mind as the memories started to trickle back. She knew that she must not tell, must not say who she was or what she was doing here. She closed her eyes and put both hands again on her stomach.

She thought of her father's wrath and her banishment to Aunt Sarah's in Devon. And she remembered how she had run away, preferring the anonymity of London to some fearsome home for bad girls in Weston.

Why had she been going there? Luke, yes, that was it. He was wounded. Aunt Sarah didn't want her to stay on her own in the house. Everything was a muddle in her mind.

Then the smaller details began to return, and she realised that she had lost her money in the bombing and if it was not found and returned to her, her security was gone. Without money what could she do? Did she want to keep this baby now? Yes, of course she wanted to keep it. But how? No home, no husband, no money, and no name!

Tears began to course down her cheeks, but at the same time a sudden iron will. And an idea. Her bruised head could be a life-line! Memory? She could say that she remembered nothing except that her husband had been killed in France. Everything else had been blotted out by the blow on her head in that blessed bomb.

This would be her story. Relief began to pour over her as the idea took root. It was a nearly perfect plan, a lie yes, but surely, with the world against her and her baby, a lie that she would be forgiven one day.

6

'My husband was killed in France.' Deborah kept repeating the words over and over again to all the well-wishers and staff who arrived every day to question her.

'But if you give us his name we can trace his records, get you some money, find your family.'

At this point Deborah would always turn her head away and refuse to answer. 'I still forget his name, and mine,' she said. She guessed they didn't believe her, but she could think of nothing else to tell them, and the bandage still around her head was a protection, an excuse for a failed memory. No trace of her bags had been found so she was registered as an unknown person. 'Your identity bracelet?' they asked frequently. 'You should have been wearing it on your wrist.'

'It must have come off,' she said faintly, remembering now that she had taken off the small silver chain engraved with her name and identity number and had hidden it in the bottom of the old suitcase when she first left Devon. She hoped now that it would never be found amongst the rubble.

At last they allowed her to get up, to walk around the wards of the big London hospital, to help with some of the other patients, and then, when it was pronounced that her wounds were quite healed and there was no more they could do for her she was called into Matron's office.

'We are sending you to a mother and baby home in Kent,' she told her. 'You have continually refused to give us any name, address, or any other details, but we have to look after you and your baby. You may be suffering from a genuine memory loss. It does sometimes happen after injuries such as yours, and if this is so, your memory will eventually return. Meanwhile you will live in the Denton House Home until your baby is born and other arrangements can be made. Are you agreeable to this?'

Deborah was amazed that she should even be asked. She nodded her head and could fell tears again in her eyes. 'I have nothing to take with me,' she whispered.

Matron indicated two large paper carriers standing on the floor. 'We have found you some maternity dresses,' she said a little more kindly now. 'And you will need a name. Surely you can remember your name?'

Deborah hesitated. She had resolutely held on to her assertion that she could remember nothing. Then suddenly, 'Margaret,' she said. 'I have remembered. It came to me last night. Margaret Smith.'

The woman sniffed and looked at her suspiciously. 'It is a very common name,' she said. 'Margaret Smith! But I suppose it will do. We shall see that you have ration books and a new identity disc in that name.'

Deborah nodded. Lying was becoming natural to her now. She felt a great wash of shame. Why was she doing all this? It had seemed the right thing to do before she came to London, but lies bred lies. Her mother had always said that, and once you went down that particular slippery slope there was no climbing back. She shivered and swayed slightly on her feet. 'Thank you, Matron,' she whispered. 'I am very grateful for all you have done for me.'

The interview was obviously at an end. Matron stood up. 'Take your bags, and I wish you well, Margaret Smith,' she said. Deborah could hear the suspicion in her voice as she repeated the name.

The mother and baby home stood outside the town of Benton and Deborah looked at its forbidding walls and great studded front door with some dismay. Yet it was a refuge. Here she would sink into anonymity, have her baby, and then decide what to do about her life.

During those autumn weeks she often thought of her parents, of Aunt Sarah, and of her cousins, Luke and Simon, and Warren, always Warren. He was somehow faintly unreal in her mind now. She could hardly recall his features, and wished desperately for a photograph.

And she was heart-breakingly home-sick.

'Why are you here if you've got a hubby?' she was asked one day as she and another girl were standing in front of huge stone sinks washing clothes.

'He's dead,' she said, wondering about the half-truth of this.

Her questioner, a girl of about her own age, turned to look at her. 'In the war?'

Deborah nodded. 'Normandy.'

'You get some money then don't you? A pension or something?'

'It hasn't come through yet.' More lies. Deborah thumped at the dresses and knickers in the sink before her. 'What about you?' she asked.

The girl grinned at her. 'I'll get nothing from him, will I? A Yank of course. Gave me loads of nylons and gum and this lot as well.' She nodded down at her bulge which was touching the sink. 'He told me about his ranch, said he'd come and get me, take me to see his old mum as soon as the war was over and we'd get married. All porkies of course. Never mind. As soon as I get rid of this little trouble I'll get a job and never trust a bloke again. Learnt my lesson the hard way.' She laughed and didn't seem to care very much about anything. Deborah envied her.

'You're going to have it adopted?'

'Sure thing. I don't want to get lumbered with a kid now do I?'

'Suppose not,' Deborah said weakly.

'It's different for you though,' the girl said. 'You got a husband, even if he's a dead 'un. You're respectable. They'll all be sorry for you, young war widow and all that. Can't think what you're doing in a place like this.'

Suddenly Deborah wished, oh how she wished, that this was true, that she was a respectable war widow, a woman with a pension, and a man's name for protection. What a fool she'd been. But her baby moved again, kicked her, and she knew that she loved it, could never give it up whatever horrors the future held. And she was also racked with guilt about what she had done to her family.

That evening she tore some sheets of paper from an old exercise book that she found lying about in the dining-room and wrote two brief and nearly identical notes.

I'm very, very sorry to have brought you all such unhappiness. I love you very much and will be in touch in the New Year. I am well and reasonably content and hope that you are. My love and best wishes to Luke and I hope he is feeling better now.

Love to you all, Deborah.

She would have to ask for envelopes and that was a dangerous undertaking, but eventually one of the girls, a new arrival in the home, managed to produce two crumpled brown ones and Deborah wrote out the addresses and posted them a few days later when she was allowed to go into town for some supplies. No stamps of course. Her mother and aunt would have to pay the extra when the letters arrived.

'Have they found your husband yet?' one of the girls asked yet again that evening. 'This place is mostly for us fallen girls with no man, not for the likes of you. What regiment was he in?'

'Can't remember,' Deborah said. 'I was in the bombing in Chiswick and my head got a real bashing, I can't remember a thing except my name.'

'What about your things?'

Deborah shrugged. 'Lost, blown to bits probably.'

The girl looked at her curiously, and Deborah realised that they were all beginning to doubt her story now. How long would she be able to keep up the pretence?

'Well, I think they ought to try a bit harder to find out who you are, bombing or no bombing.'

Deborah was suddenly frightened. If only she hadn't begun this great subterfuge of lies she could be back in Devon with Aunt Sarah, and perhaps Luke. She shuddered however and knew that she couldn't face Luke while she so obviously carried Warren's baby. Yes, it was stupid perhaps, but that was how she felt.

But how were they all? What about Luke's war injuries? And Simon? Was there any news of him? She knew nothing about all the people she loved most in the world. And most important of all, what about her mother? A great well of guilt opened in her heart.

But constantly she thought of Warren, the cause of everything. Had he been wounded too? If so he'd be back in America now. Did he think of her at all? Most likely he had not survived that first horrific push into Normandy. Even if he had, she would probably never see him again. She tried very hard to be realistic.

December brought thoughts of Christmas and a sense of gloom prevailed in the Denton Mother and Baby Home. 'We've got to make flipping paper chains,' someone said as they looked at the box of coloured paper strips that had been dumped on one of the tables. 'Reminds me of the Infants Room at flipping school.'

In spite of their moans, they all survived Christmas, ate roast rabbit and a wartime variety of pudding made largely of carrots, and the garish paper chains hung limply above their heads. Deborah felt that she would remember this Christmas forever.

On the last day of 1944 Deborah began to feel her first pains. She clenched her teeth and wondered if perhaps at last the long months of waiting were over. The big battle of her life, both that of giving birth and of knowing what to do about it afterwards, was about to begin. Or was this just a bout of colic? Had she eaten something disagreeable? Not an unlikely thing to do nowadays and in this place, she thought.

She lay in the unyielding bed clutching the blanket in rigid hands trying not to cry out, but eventually she could bear the searing pain no longer.

'I'm dying, I'm dying, help me,' she screamed, and then Matron arrived, all starched uniform and efficiency.

'Rubbish, child,' she said. 'It'll be a long time yet. Gather your things up and I'll get you taken up the road.'

'Up the road' was the euphemism for the grim little ward of the cottage hospital where all the babies from the home were delivered. Deborah staggered to her feet and looked around despairingly. 'I can't,' she managed. 'I can't do anything.'

Matron pulled an ancient carpet bag from the top of the cupboard. The suitcase had never been recovered and Deborah had found this bag at a surplus stall in the local market. She had bargained for it, and eventually had paid threepence.

Matron looked at it with distaste and wrinkled her nose, but she plonked it on to the bed. 'Of course you can. Nightdress, toothbrush, baby things, that's all you'll need.'

Baby things? Deborah had none of those. She pulled her nightdress from beneath her pillow, then doubled up over the bed again as another pain tore through her protesting body.

She finally managed to push various things into the bag and then found herself being led out of the building which had become her refuge during the past weeks, down the road and into the gloomy red-brick maternity ward, a place which had always held a sense of foreboding for the girls of the mother and baby home.

None of them were prepared for what went on there. No-one returning with a closely wrapped crying baby would mention a word. 'Mustn't say,' they would whisper when asked. 'Not allowed.'

Once inside the building she was ushered to a bed in a small ward, bidden to get undressed and then told that she would have a bath. The hot water calmed her, and to her surprise she felt comforted. She lay there in some sort of stupor until a nurse who looked much younger than she did, helped her out, helped to dry her, and then gave her a flowing white gown open down the back.

The very sight of it terrified Deborah. It resembled the shroud that had been prepared years ago for her grandmother. But she was beyond caring now, and when eventually she was left quite alone on a hard high bed to cope with her increasing pain she gave herself up to her screams and her terror.

Nightmare hours of darkness followed, with only the flickering gas light for company and she seemed to float in and out of consciousness, aware only of the fierce agony of her body.

'Bear down. Push,' the voices came from a long distance, from a tunnel of great darkness. Then there was another sound, a protesting baby's wail. She came suddenly from the depths of horror to blessed relief in what seemed like one glorious moment. Her young body was triumphant and at peace at last.

'A cup of tea?' Gentle arms helped her sit up, held a cup to her lips. 'You have a very pretty little girl,' the nurse said. 'With lots of fair hair. A 1945 baby. It'll be victory year so she's a victory baby.'

Deborah smiled at the idea, and sipped the welcome liquid and turned to look for her baby. After what seemed like a very long time a small bundle was handed to her and she saw a small red face bordered by some blonde fluff.

She pushed at the confining shawl, and stared at the big blue eyes that appeared to be studying her with angry intent. Deborah burst into tears. How would she ever manage to give up this child? But equally how would she ever manage to keep her? Love was forbidden, but love came in unbidden waves, sweeping over her, and her tears fell on to her baby's face.

During the next two weeks Deborah fought against loving her child, but she was supposed to be a war widow, there was no question of the baby being given for adoption as happened to the babies of most of the other girls in the home. 'You're lucky,' some of them said. 'You're respectable. What are you going to call her?'

'Victoria,' Deborah said without previous thought. 'She is to be Victoria. Like you say, this is going to be victory year.'

'Have you anywhere to go?' Matron said when the obligatory two weeks of rest and recuperation were over. 'You can't stay here of course now that your baby is born. Have you remembered anything yet? If not then you will have to go to a mental hospital where you can be treated.'

Immediately huge alarm bells sounded in Deborah's mind. Mental ward? Mental hospital? The sort of institution where her baby would be spirited away, and where she would be imprisoned for the rest of her life.

She would have to tell more lies, invent an address and relatives if she was to escape the enormous clutches of the authorities. She had sudden visions of vast wards, of white gowned doctors clipping various pieces of fearsome equipment to her head, and of actually going out of her mind.

Anything was better than that, even her father's wrath. Perhaps the truth might be better after all. She hung her head in shame and despair. All her grand ideas of subterfuge had landed her in this terrible mess, this frightful dilemma.

'Sit down, Margaret Smith,' Matron said indicating a chair at the other side of her vast desk. She stressed the name and Deborah knew that it would always cause disbelief. 'It's not Margaret Smith is it?' the woman probed. 'You are not Margaret Smith at all are you?'

7

Deborah shook her head. 'No,' she admitted. 'My name is Deborah Jenkins. I have no husband. My parents live in Bristol.' There was a long silence and Deborah stood immobile staring at the ground. She felt frightened and very alone. What would happen to her and to her baby now?

When she dared to look up she saw that Matron was shuffling some papers on her desk. But her voice when she spoke was kind in spite of the harsh judgement.

'I guessed as much,' she said. 'You have deceived the authorities, your parents, and of course, yourself, Deborah. We shall now have to contact your parents. If they agree to take you in again after your disgrace you will be given fresh documents, a ration book and travel warrant, and we shall see that you are sent safely home. Your baby will remain here for adoption.'

'No,' Deborah said with quiet determination. 'Not adoption, please. I want to keep her.' She clasped her hands in anguish. 'I will do anything you ask, but please allow me to keep her.'

'And how do you propose to do that? You are obviously a well educated girl. You should go back to school and continue your studies. It will be in the baby's interests too, to have a proper family with respectably married parents. Keeping her will be very selfish indeed.'

Deborah groped in her apron pocket for a handkerchief. 'My mother might help me,' she said.

'That's not impossible of course. You would have to learn to think of the child as your sister if your mother agreed to adopt her. It often happens. We will contact your parents immediately.' She pushed a piece of paper and pencil across the desk. 'Write your name and address here,' she said. 'And no lies this time.'

Deborah took the pencil in trembling fingers and slowly wrote the words that would condemn her again to her father's wrath and her mother's shame. She handed it over and then stood up straight and her breath came in long shuddering gasps. 'How long will it take?' she asked.

'It depends on how quickly they respond,' Matron said. 'I will write immediately. We may hear before the end of the week.' She stood up. 'And I will just say, in my letter, that you were wounded in a bomb attack and lost your memory,' she added. And then, as an afterthought, 'I have absolutely no idea what you were doing in London, but that's something you must sort out with your parents. I shall not mention it.'

Deborah stared at her in grateful surprise and thought she saw the ghost of a smile on her face. 'Thank you, thank you, Matron,' she said. 'And my baby?' The question hung in the air like a threatening bomb waiting to explode around her head.

'That remains to be seen. I shall let you know.'

Deborah stumbled out of the room and back to her dormitory. She sat on her bed for a long time. What had she done? How was she to explain London? How could she have decided so rapidly on this course of action? Her father's remembered face filled her with fear, but with anger too. He would surely force her to give up her baby. But there was nothing she could do now.

All the decisions of her life would be made for her. In revealing the truth she had given up her freedom to decide her own fate and that of Victoria, but then, she thought miserably, what freedom did a sixteen-year-old girl with a baby born out of wedlock have anyway?

She cried again, then looked at the clock on the wall. Nearly six o'clock, and feeds must be given regularly on the hour even if the world was falling apart and your heart was breaking. She wiped her eyes and made her way to the baby room.

Victoria was awake, her tiny dimpled arms waving in the air and Deborah took her from her coat and unbuttoned her blouse. She held her tightly, overwhelmed with love. Could anyone anywhere force her to give up this precious part of herself? Yes, she knew that they could.

She wanted to run outside with Victoria clasped in her arms far away from authority and cruel laws. But she had done that once before and she knew now that running away from your life led to nowhere, nowhere at all. She had made her decision and there was no changing her mind now.

For better or for worse she had told the truth at last, and whatever happened to her and her baby was completely out of her hands. Tears trickled from her eyes again and fell gently on to her baby's face.

★　★　★

Deborah's father was waiting for her on Temple Meads Station. She had been told that he would be there, that her mother was ill, too ill to come. Matron had explained that it was only because of her mother's pleadings, and because of her illness, that the baby was to go home with her. The adoption would be arranged in Bristol. Deborah had not been able to find out any more than that.

He stood on the platform, trilby set squarely on his head, and a grim look on his face. She saw him from the train window and her heart raced with apprehension.

'Want some help?' The young man in sailor's uniform who had been sitting opposite her for most of the journey from London stood up and took her old carpet bag from the rack above their heads. 'Careful now,' he said. He glanced at the baby in her arms. 'Nice kid, good too.'

'Thanks,' Deborah muttered. 'Yes I'd like a hand.'

He carried the bag on to the platform for her. 'Good luck,' he said. 'Lucky guy, your hubby.' He put the bag down and grinned. 'I'd better get back on board. Wouldn't like the outfit to go without me. The navy wouldn't be very pleased. You all right now?'

She nodded and managed a smile.

Then he was gone, and she was alone among the thronging uncaring crowds, alone except for the child in her arms, and her father bearing down fiercely upon her. They stood and looked at each other.

'Dad,' she managed at last. 'Thank you for coming.'

He looked her up and down. 'Come on,' he said briefly. He picked up her bag. 'Best get going. I don't like leaving your mother for too long.'

Wordlessly she followed him down the subway and out of the station. There was a bus waiting and she was surprised that he stood back and allowed her to board first. She found a double seat and with difficulty managed to slide over to the window side. Thankfully Victoria was still sound asleep and Deborah wondered when her father would take a first look at his granddaughter. Granddaughter! She surprised herself with the word. She had not thought of it before and it gave her a small stab of both wonder and grief.

'Two to Ashley Down,' he said to the bus conductor while he fished in his pocket for the right change. Then he turned to look at Deborah, but carefully kept his eyes averted from the sleeping baby. 'You've nearly brought your mother to the grave with worry,' he muttered. 'Now you'll have to look after her.'

'What's the matter with her?' Deborah asked. 'Dad, please tell me. She's not going to die is she?' The thought was so terrible that she closed her eyes with the horror of it. If her mother died she would be guilty. If her wickedness, as her father called it, had brought her mother so much suffering, how would she ever manage to live any meaningful sort of life again?

But as the misery of it all swirled around in her mind she thought again that even now, she was still thinking of herself, of how she would cope, how to go on living.

Her father stared at her. 'We don't know,' he said. 'She caught the 'flu and couldn't shake it off, and now it sounds to me like pneumonia. She's been worried out of her head by your running away and not knowing where you were. She wants to see the baby though. Can't imagine why, but that's what she wants.'

They were silent for the rest of the journey, neither having anything at all that they could bear to say to each other. When the bus eventually stopped at the end of the road where Deborah had lived all her life, her father retrieved the bag and made his way to the door. He didn't look back, didn't help her out, just stepped from the bus platform and waited for her.

At that moment Victoria chose to open her eyes and yell, and for one second Deborah's father glanced down at the closely wrapped bundle in his daughter's arms. 'Got a dummy or something?' he questioned. There was irritation in his voice.

Deborah hastily plugged up the tiny crying mouth. 'She's hungry,' she said, and then blushed, wondering how she would manage to breast feed her baby without embarrassment in this home in which she'd only ever been a carefree schoolgirl. She counted on her mother's understanding and help. Please God she was not too ill to give it.

The house looked just as it had when she last saw it back in the summer. It seemed like a hundred years ago. The privet hedge that bordered the small front garden was neatly clipped, the same net curtains adorned the bay windows, and the brass step below the front door gleamed as if newly polished. Deborah glanced down at it as her father put his key in the lock and wondered who did all the housework now. Was her mother well enough? She would soon know.

A round smiling face greeted her as soon as she stepped inside. 'Aunt Sarah,' she said, and her spirits lifted as though the sun had suddenly reappeared behind grey stormy clouds. 'No-one told me that you would be here.'

'Didn't they, love? I expect they thought it might worry you. But your mum needed someone. Men are no good at times like this.' She kissed Deborah warmly and then looked down at the closely wrapped bundle in her arms. 'Can I see the babe?' She gently pulled aside the confining shawl and her finger traced the tiny forehead. 'She's lovely, a perfect little darling.'

'Where's Mummy?' After her first pleasure at seeing her aunt, Deborah had become alarmed that her mother was not there to greet her.

'In bed.'

The stark words were terrifying.

'Can I go up?'

'Just for a minute,' Sarah said. 'Give the baby to me. I'll hold her till you come down and we can all get settled. There's a nice cup of tea just made. I expect you're both tired and hungry.'

'Can't I take Victoria up?'

'Not just now, love. Wait a bit. See how she is.'

More alarmed than ever Deborah gave the baby into her aunt's arms and ran up the stairs two at a time.

Pamela Jenkins lay on one side of the big double bed and when she saw Deborah she opened her eyes and smiled. 'Deborah, darling. Is it really you?' She struggled to free herself from the confining sheet. 'I've been so worried for so long.'

Deborah was shocked and desperately ashamed and devoid of speech for a moment. She took her mother's hands in hers at first not quite knowing what to do, and then she knelt at the bedside and clasped the frail body as closely as she could. 'Mummy, oh

Mummy,' she whispered. 'Can you ever forgive me?'

'There's nothing to forgive,' Pamela whispered. 'Nothing at all. We were too hard on you, your father and I. I should have been firmer, stood up to him. But now you're here, and that's all that matters, and the baby too. Is the baby here?'

'Downstairs with Aunt Sarah.'

'What have you called her?'

'Victoria Pamela,' Deborah said hastily adding her mother's name. 'She's not been christened yet, but those will be her names. Victoria for victory and Pamela for you, Mummy.'

Her mother smiled. 'Bring her to see me soon, Debbie love,' she whispered. Deborah didn't spring up immediately but just knelt there until her mother's eyes closed, and then she saw that Aunt Sarah was standing in the doorway.

'Leave her now, dear. She sleeps a lot, and that's the best cure,' she whispered. 'Come and have a cup of tea and see to your babe.'

Deborah extricated herself from her mother's arms and tiptoed from the room. Once outside the door she turned to her aunt. 'She is going to get better isn't she, Aunt Sarah?'

'We're all praying that she will,' Sarah said. 'But she has been very ill, she still is. But now come and see my little surprise.'

Mystified Deborah followed her down the stairs and into the seldom-used front room of the house. It was usually cold and forbidding but today there was a fire in the grate.

And there, standing beneath the window was a pram, a white and black Silver Cross, with four great wheels, and big chromium springs. She rushed across and looked down, and saw her baby resplendent in its frilled interior, dummy plugged firmly into her little mouth. Deborah picked her up and hugged her. 'Aunt Sarah, where did such a wonderful pram come from?'

'From a friend,' she said mysteriously. 'It's just on loan. And a terrible job I had to bring it up here on the train. Your father was not best pleased when it was delivered here by the railway van. But I was determined to do something to welcome you both home.'

Deborah hugged her. 'You're really wonderful, Aunt. I'm so so grateful. I'd better feed her,' she said, embarrassed now. 'Where shall I go?'

'I've prepared the little back bedroom for you,' Sarah said. 'I'm in your room for now as it's nearer your mother in case she needs me in the night.'

The little room at the back of the house looked out on the tiny garden and beyond that were the great grey buildings of the Muller's Orphanage, a constant reminder of the possible fate of children with no parents.

Earlier in the war they had been evacuated to the country and troops of various descriptions had been billeted there from time to time. The last had of course been the Americans. All gone now, to fight against Hitler's once conquering armies.

Deborah put a now protesting Victoria on the bed, threw off her coat, unbuttoned her blouse and then sat down in the little nursing chair that had probably been used when she herself was a baby.

As she sat in the quiet room all the stresses and problems of the last year ran like some harrowing newsreel through her brain, and the final grief was her mother's illness.

She wondered how she would possibly manage on her own here when Aunt Sarah left, as she surely would eventually. How could she cope with an invalid mother, a difficult father, and a young baby?

⋆　⋆　⋆

Two days later, as Allied bombs annihilated the ancient city of Dresden, and as Canadian and American soldiers pressed on towards the Rhine in their efforts to free Europe and end the war, so it was that in the little house in

Bristol, none of these great events seemed of any importance at all, for at midnight Pamela Jenkins died quietly in her sleep.

She had seen her granddaughter, had summoned enough strength to kiss her.

'She's beautiful,' she had whispered. 'Look after her and your father, Debbie.'

How Deborah managed to get through the next week she would never know. The days passed in a blur of preparing food that no-one wanted, talking to endless friends and relatives, many of them almost complete strangers, dealing with flowers, and the funeral service itself, and of course, feeding her baby. Those moments alone with her tiny daughter were a blessed relief from all the harrowing events going on downstairs.

And when it was all over, the guests departed, the house quiet and sombre again except for Victoria's occasional wails, then Deborah's fears returned. What to do now? How to cope? Her mother was not here with the offer of adoption, the lifeline she had hoped would be thrown to her, and Aunt Sarah was saying now, that she must go home, that Luke would be needing her.

Deborah waited for an invitation to return to Devon with her, but none came. When she thought of Luke all alone in the house by the sea she longed to be there. Now that her figure had returned to almost normal she was feeling less ashamed to face him and eventually she plucked up the courage to confront her aunt with the burning question.

'Can I come and visit you, Aunt Sarah? I should dearly love to see Luke again after so long.'

'In time, deary. When the babe is a bit bigger and your father has got over his grief. But you're needed here just now aren't you?'

Deborah had to agree that she was, but when she thought about being alone with her father and baby in this house her spirits dropped to her boots. Yet of course this was what was expected of her.

She must become a housewife without a husband. Suddenly she longed to be young and carefree again but that part of her life seemed to have gone for ever.

With every passing day after Aunt Sarah had left for Devon, Deborah's father became more and more morose. Each morning he would sit at the breakfast table without speaking unless there was something spectacular in the newspaper, in which case he would read it aloud, pronouncing vehemently on the item's value in the imminent downfall of Germany.

When the US First Army reached and crossed the Rhine his mood changed and he was ecstatic for a time. Deborah was both amazed and thrilled to see that his depression seemed to be lifting.

'They're of some use after all,' he said when he had finished reading the report. 'Your Yanks. Putting up a jolly good show in France, and now Germany.'

Deborah's heart leapt momentarily. Your Yanks he had said, it made her think of Warren. She had tried to put him out of her mind lately. She took the newspaper herself when he had finished with it.

So the Americans were in Cologne now. She knew nothing of Cologne, but just to think of Warren there in the triumphant drive through the ruined streets gave her a little frisson of pleasure. Perhaps after all? Perhaps one day?

But she folded the paper, put it in the coal house on the pile of others ready for making paper sticks to light the fire, fed Victoria and put her in her beautiful pram beneath the front room window, and prepared to go out to do the shopping.

'I should love to take the baby with me,' she said wistfully to her father knowing quite well what his answer would be. She was not allowed to take the pram outside. Her father had decreed that although the neighbours knew perfectly well that she had come home with a baby, none of them must see her.

This ill-begotten child must not be pushed triumphantly along the street in the pram fit for royalty, nor in any pram for that matter. Brian Jenkins was still adamant that she must be adopted one day soon and he wanted no complications.

'No,' he said. 'You leave her here with me and she'll come to no harm. You go and get the rations.' It was the Saturday agreement.

When he was not at work then Deborah would stand in the queues and bring in the provisions.

Resigned, she pulled on her old school winter coat, tied the belt firmly at her waist and took a basket and several folded paper carriers. 'There's a dummy tucked down inside the pram,' she said.

She often wondered what happened when she left her father with Victoria. Did he just leave her alone and refuse to look at her, or did he perhaps creep in and rock the pram on its great springy wheels? She hoped it was the latter, but he always refused to comment in any detail when she returned.

'She's OK,' he would usually say in reply to her worried enquiries. 'Good kid, no trouble.' It was the only compliment she had ever heard from him.

This particular Saturday the queues were longer than usual, the provisions meagre, but Deborah was grateful to be able to buy a rabbit, still with its fur on it was true, but none the worse for that except for the forlorn expression on its little dead face. 'All fresh,' the butcher told her. 'My boy trapped it last night.'

When she had finished buying as many provisions as the rations would allow Deborah hurried as fast as she could to get home. She pushed open the front door and called to her father triumphantly.

'I managed to get a rabbit, Dad. You'll have to skin it, then I'll make a stew for tonight.' She dumped her shopping on the kitchen table, washed her hands, and went into the front room to get Victoria. She crossed to the pram and looked down at its empty blankets. Unbelieving she pulled at them. The dummy was gone too.

'Dad,' she screamed. 'Have you got Victoria?' She rushed through the house, but there was no sign of either of them. She went into the back garden and stared around at the bedraggled Brussels sprout plants and at the soggy lawn. 'Dad,' she shouted, 'Where are you?'

She ran up the stairs two at a time and flung open all the bedroom doors. Nothing! Then she stared at the open drawers of the chest in which she kept Victoria's clothes and all the folded snowy white terry-towelling napkins.

They were completely empty. There was nothing there except the newspaper linings.

She stood for a moment and then charged downstairs again, returned to the pram and threw out the blankets in a frenzy as though Victoria might indeed be still there hidden beneath them.

Finally she went into the road and stared helplessly up and down at the other houses. Then she walked slowly back into the house and sat down on the settee beside the empty pram.

When she thought about this terrible moment in all the months that followed Deborah couldn't be sure how long she sat there. Time was of no consequence, nothing was of any consequence any more.

If Victoria had been taken from her then she might as well die right here and now.

A key in the lock and her father's entrance brought her violently from her state of shock. Had he done it? Had he?

How could he have allowed such a terrible thing to happen?

'Where is she,' she gasped as he took off his hat and set it carefully on the top of the hall stand. 'Where's Victoria?'

8

Her father's slow methodical actions
drove her to near frenzy. 'It's for the
best,' he said. 'She'll have a better home
than we could ever give her. The
Welfare came and took her when you
were out. They have a lot of folk
wanting to adopt babies. It's for the
best, Deborah, trust me.'

She threw herself at him then, beat
her fists on his chest so that he had to
hold her firmly. 'I hate you,' she
screamed. 'I hate you. How could you
do this to me? Where's the Welfare
office? I'll go now and get her back. I
haven't given my permission. They
can't do it.'

'You're underage,' he said as he
disentangled himself from her angry
arms. 'Now be a sensible girl and come
and have a cup of tea and I'll tell you
more about the arrangements. It's my

decision, Deborah. You're only a child yourself and therefore I have to decide what is best for you and the baby.'

He took off his coat and put it on a thick padded hanger and then walked past her into the kitchen. 'I went with them. I saw her safely installed in the baby home. She'll be fine.'

'Baby home?' She screamed. 'This is her home. I'm her mother.'

'She'll be fostered until she's chosen by a good and respectable family.'

Deborah was speechless with fury and grief. She couldn't sit meekly down and drink tea and listen to his reasons and excuses. She ran up to her room and threw herself on to the bed and soaked the pillow with her helpless tears. She knew that what he said was perfectly true. She'd heard it from other girls. Until the magic day of your twenty-first birthday you were utterly defenceless and dependent.

Her breasts were heavy with milk and the pain and the seeping wetness made her distress more difficult to bear. Then she was suddenly filled with determination and resolve.

Slowly she got up, splashed cold water on to her face, put on her coat and crept down the stairs and outside into the street. Where should she go? She knew that her mother's doctor lived in the next road. That perhaps was he first place to try.

She stumbled from the house in even greater distress. The Parish Church with its Vicarage was just around the corner. Perhaps there she might find some help and comfort? But no, the opinion was the same.

The Vicar stared at her disapprovingly. 'You cannot bring up a baby with he stigma of illegitimacy on her head,' he said sternly. 'Your father was thinking of the child. He asked my advice and I told him that if she has a good home with two loving parents, then she will be far better off than being brought up by a schoolgirl. The idea is totally preposterous.'

He blew his nose vociferously. 'All

this worry, coming on top of your mother's death, has upset him very much. You must do your best to comfort him, Deborah.'

Comfort him indeed! She felt more like killing him. Deborah stomped indignantly out of the Vicarage and took the bus to the town centre. She asked a policeman and then a passing nun if they knew the address of the welfare.

She went into the general post office, but the man there looked at her suspiciously and told her to go home. She spent the whole of the afternoon searching without any success, and eventually she went unwillingly back to the empty pram and the empty cot.

But the pram was nowhere to be seen. She stormed through the house. 'What have you done with the pram?' she said. It was the final betrayal.

He was in the back garden planting some early vegetables in the small border at the end of the lawn. He stood up and flinched, one hand rubbing his back. 'I've sent it back to your aunt,' he said wearily. 'It belonged to her neighbour.'

'How? How did you get rid of it so quickly?'

'The same way it came. By rail.'

And then she knew that it must have all been arranged beforehand. He knew that Victoria would be taken away today, and he had ordered the railway freight collection van to take the pram too.

How could he have deceived her so? How could he have done such a terrible thing to his own granddaughter?

'I'm sorry if I seem hard,' he said. 'Had your mother lived it might have been different. We could have adopted the baby as ours, but that's impossible now. Life will be difficult enough as things are. And think of the shame Victoria would suffer when she was old enough to understand.

'Just think of her and not of yourself for once.'

'I am thinking of Victoria,' she screamed, 'it's me she needs, her mother, her real mother, not some couple who'll never manage to love her as I do.'

'Wrong, you're quite wrong,' he said. 'You think that you love her at the moment, but soon you'll forget all about her, and when you're a bit older you'll get married and have other kids.'

'Never,' Deborah said. 'I'll never forget her as long as I live.' She turned away from him and went inside. She felt totally devoid of all emotion, an empty shell out of which all life and love had been plucked and destroyed. She sat on her bed and stared out of the window at the great orphanage buildings.

Orphans! She had seen them over the wall every day before they had been evacuated to the country. She had shuddered and pitied them, and had been constantly grateful for her home, for the fact that she had two loving parents.

Suddenly she felt less sure of herself. Could her father possibly be right about Victoria? Was it important for a child to have proper married parents, a father and a mother and a secure home? Everyone seemed to think so. Was she, Deborah, being selfish as he said? Could she be thinking just of herself yet again?

She had never heard of any girls of her age bringing up a baby on their own without a mother to give help and support. Victoria deserved the best that could be found for her. That was definitely true.

The worm of doubt in her own judgements curled around her heart and her anger began to abate a little. Maybe after all, the adults she had spoken to were more capable of making life and death decisions, and although her heart was breaking perhaps she should submit and hope that one day life would smile again. She strongly doubted it at this moment but, reluctantly, she went downstairs.

Her father was just coming in wearily from the garden. She stood and watched him wash his hands in the old scullery sink, and then sit down at the table in his usual place. He looked old and defeated.

Unwillingly she felt a glimmer of pity for him penetrate her icy heart. Could she manage to find a small measure of forgiveness? And might she even try to give him some love and comfort? He was suffering too she realised, and she had been so taken up with her own life, that she had hardly been aware of his continual grieving for her mother.

'What do you want for tea?' The words were forced and she saw him look up at her, surprised. 'The rabbit will do for tomorrow,' she said. She knew that she couldn't face that little dead thing tonight. 'I managed to get some bacon this morning as well. I'll fry that and there's bubble and squeak from yesterday.'

Yesterday! Yesterday was a whole world away. She had Victoria then and as long as her baby was in her arms she had felt strong and able to face the world and whatever it had in store.

She tried to keep some good thoughts about her father uppermost in her mind but as she set the meal on the table she knew that to forgive him completely would be one of the hardest things she had ever done. She stared at her plate and felt physically sick.

The next few days passed in a grey blur. Her father was obviously trying to forget the past and look forward instead of back, but they seldom spoke except about the war. 'The end can't be far away,' he said a few days later at breakfast as he spread the newspaper out on the table.

He was always saying it just as though speaking these optimistic words would make them come true a little sooner and would make everything else all right too. 'Germany is being given a good bashing by the allies,' he added.

Deborah didn't reply. She finished her corn flakes and then carried the dishes through to the scullery, washed them up in the stone sink and started washing vegetables. Perhaps if she only voiced the good things too, then life would change for her as well.

She glanced at the carrots that her father had brought home from his allotment the previous evening. They were fresh and healthy and coated with the soft brown earth that had produced such a wealth of good food during all the years of shortages and rationing.

'Nice carrots,' she proclaimed and then wanted to laugh bitterly. Was that the only pleasant thing she could think to say? 'You've done a good job with the allotment, Dad,' she added. 'We've never gone short of vegetables have we?'

He looked at her in surprise. 'I suppose we haven't. Dig for victory and all that. Well, it was all I could do wasn't it? Too old to fight. Got to keep going somehow. Sorry they're so muddy.'

Deborah was surprised at the little glow of satisfaction that even such a small compliment produced in both herself and in her father. She resolved to make more effort in future.

She knew that she could never forgive him for what he had done, but the pity she felt for him would sometimes produce small results. She sometimes tried to cook one of his favourite dishes with the few rations she managed to find. It meant endlessly standing in queues, but the triumph of half a pound of sausages or a bit of tripe was worth it.

Gradually as the news of the war began to get more hopeful she saw that her father was slightly less gloomy and sometimes he even smiled and thanked her as he ate one of her concoctions.

'Could you press the trousers of my best suit?' he said surprisingly one day.

She had no idea how to do such a thing but she would try. 'I don't know that I'll be able to do it very well, but I'll do my best,' she said doubtfully. 'When are you going to wear it, Dad?'

'Saturday, a do at work,' he said mysteriously.

'Oh?' Deborah hoped for some more

information, but none was forthcoming. She had been surprised to see him go out in this seldom used garment last Saturday as well. Before that it had not been out of the wardrobe since her mother's funeral.

However, feeling very curious she went into his bedroom the next day and pulled it from the rail. The weather was windy and bright for April so she hung the jacket on the washing line to freshen it up.

Then she took the two irons, put them on the stove, lit the gas beneath each one and found the pressing cloth that her mother had used. She dampened it and laid the trousers on the old wooden board that did for most of the ironing.

As she pressed, the trousers steamed and the irons seemed to sizzle. There was a faint smell rising from them and she sniffed, trying to remember what it could be. It was not mothballs which she had expected, but was something slightly pleasanter. With the trousers done as carefully as she could manage she put them on their hanger and took them out into the back-garden to join the jacket on the line.

It was then that she saw the paper, a bit of blue deckle-edged paper sticking out from one of the jacket pockets. Paper such as her mother had used on her occasional letters to Aunt Sarah. What use could her father have for such 'feminine fripperies', as she had heard him call this matching paper and envelopes which her mother liked?

She took it out of the pocket and unfolded it. But it was not her mother's paper. She could see that. Similar, but not the same. And it was certainly not her mother's writing. Feeling slightly guilty but unable now to fold the paper and put it back in the pocket without satisfying her curiosity, she read,

Dear Howard,
I was so grateful for last Saturday. Since Don was killed I have felt very sad and lonely. You have given me a

little happiness again.
With love and gratitude,
Mabel

Deborah stared at it in disbelief. Who was Mabel? Dear Howard! She had called him by his Christian name, a familiarity that only her mother and some close relations were allowed to use. Last Saturday? She tried to remember what her father had done last Saturday. Yes, he had gone out wearing this very suit, in itself a remarkable event, but she had been so wrapped up in her own grief that she had not cared, or thought to inquire where he had been.

What was he doing receiving letters from some woman who sent her love and who called him Howard? She wanted to screw the paper up into a tight ball and throw it on to the fire.

Her precious mother's memory had been violated. Then common sense prevailed. Instead she carefully inserted it back into her father's jacket pocket, and left it there on the washing line to air in the sunshine.

In the kitchen she sat curled up in the big chair by the fireside and her thoughts were a jumble of tangled emotions. Yes, the more she considered, the more she realised that her father had been slightly less gloomy lately.

If she thought of it at all then she had put it down to the success of the push into France and Germany by the allies. But was there a more personal reason?

As the sun went behind a cloud and the April skies began to darken she fetched the suit on its heavy wooden hanger and carried it upstairs to her father's wardrobe.

She opened the old oak doors and sniffed critically. There it was again, the scent she had imagined had risen from the trousers as she pressed them with the damp cloth. Lavender! Yes it was lavender.

She examined the shirts carefully. There were only four, all of them prewar. One was for Sundays and the others for everyday. She looked at the sober collection of ties hanging over a piece of string that was fixed to the inside of the door. And then she saw it.

Amongst the greys and browns was another, altogether brighter. She lifted it out and held it to the fading light from the window. She had never seen it before and still there was that faint evocative scent of lavender.

As far as she knew her father had never worn it. It was certainly not the kind of tie her mother would have chosen. Pamela Jenkins had hated lavender too. 'An old ladies' scent,' Debbie remembered her mother saying. She had a precious bottle of Coty's L'aiment, her only luxury, and Deborah knew that she herself would never be able to use any of this her mother's favourite perfume.

At least this unknown 'Mabel' wouldn't intrude on those evocative memories. Lavender was much more acceptable. But totally alarming nevertheless.

'What am I thinking of?' Deborah said to herself with a jolt. She replaced the bright offending tie. 'Am I even entertaining the idea that my father might be seeing someone, a lady friend, so soon after Mummy died?'

Here she felt tears threatening again. What must she do? Hide this awful wounding knowledge? Pretend that she had never seen the letter?

She stumbled downstairs and mechanically started to prepare the evening meal. No, she could never do that.

She felt too wounded by the recent events of her life to have any ability to cope with more deception.

As she cooked, the idea grew in her mind. Yes, he must have a new woman. Tears flowed into the bowl of potatoes.

When her father came in from work she tried to appear normal but she found it almost impossible to talk to him. The meal progressed largely in silence until he got up from the table and with careful elaboration pushed his chair into its place.

'Thank you, Deborah,' he said. 'I enjoyed that very much. You are becoming a good cook. Almost as good as your mother.' He seated himself before the fire, took out his pipe and opened the newspaper. 'Anything wrong?' he inquired. 'You're rather quiet.'

She wanted to shout at him, bang her fists on the table, even throw something, but she did none of those things. Her mother was not long dead and here he was talking about her cooking for goodness sake. And he was already seeing another woman. Deborah's anger grew by the minute. And there was the final unforgivable thing.

Thanks to this man little Victoria, her precious baby, was goodness knows where. It was monstrous, all of it, not to be borne. She didn't reply to his anxious question but hurried out of the room, banging the door behind her. She ran up the stairs two at a time and shut herself in her bedroom. Once again her pillow was soon wet with her tears.

Through her grief and anger she heard him plodding up the creaking stairway. He walked along the small landing and then, silence. She wiped her eyes and sat up on the bed wondering what he was doing. His knock on her door was timid, hardly heard, and she waited a few moments and then called, 'Come in!'

She didn't want him to come in. She felt she couldn't bear to look at him. He had taken her baby away with no thought of her feelings, no idea at all of how desperate she felt, and now he was thinking only of his own happiness. Surely he should go on being miserable, suffer with her, if that was how he thought it should be. But obviously not. If he dared bring another woman to fill her mother's place so soon it would make her own grief even harder to bear.

She sat up on the bed, her face white and angry and her fists clenched into tight balls. 'What do you want?' she managed icily.

'You're not still punishing me for that baby are you?'

'Punishing you? Of course I am. Who else should I punish?'

'Your Yank of course, and your own stupidity.'

This wasn't at all how she wanted the conversation to go. Here he was, accusing her for her misery all over again when she wanted to accuse him. She thought that at least he had come to terms with what he called 'her sin'. Her unhappiness was all his fault. If she had to lose Warren, at least she thought she could have had his baby to love.

She closed her eyes in despair and decided in that moment that she must leave, pack up her things and leave this house and her father for ever. Then, if he wanted to become involved with another woman and forget her mother she wouldn't be here to see his treachery or to spoil things for him any more.

She groped for her handkerchief and wiped her eyes. 'I'm going away,' she said. 'All I'm doing here is being a skivvy for you. You can get your fancy woman to cook your meals and wash your clothes in future. I never want to see you again.' She stood up. 'And I hope she cooks as well as Mummy!' It was the final barb and she hoped it hurt him greatly.

He looked at her in alarm. 'What do you mean, Deborah, fancy woman?'

'Just what I say. I found a letter in your pocket and your things smell of lavender, and there's a ghastly new tie with your old ones.'

It was his turn now to appear wretched. He looked round for a chair, pushed some clothes aside that were in a heap on its seat, and slumped down upon it.

'I should have told you,' he said. 'Her name is Mabel Greenslade.'

'How long has my mother been dead?' Deborah thundered the words at him. 'How could you? How could you do such a thing?'

He put his hands over his eyes

momentarily and then looked up at his daughter. 'I need some comfort in my life,' he said. 'I know that you've been making an effort to keep cheerful, Deborah, and I'm grateful, but believe me, you've often got a face as long as a fiddle.'

'And whose fault is that?' she said. 'After what you've done to me and my baby I wonder if I shall ever smile again.'

He looked at her for a long moment and then cradled his head in his hands but Deborah had not finished. 'Anyway, I'm going. I don't want to see this house or you ever again.'

'Wait a while, Deborah. Please wait for a week or so. I promise you that I have other things in my mind apart from my own happiness.'

'What do you mean?' she asked, suddenly alert for anything that might give her hope.

'Mabel and I have worked together in the office for many years,' he said. 'Your mother knew her well and liked her. I feel that she would approve, would want to see us happy again.'

He picked up a photograph of his wife which Deborah had placed in a silver frame. It was on the small table beside the chair on which he was sitting. He looked at it for a long time, traced Pamela's features gently with his fingers and then put it down gently.

Beside it was the only snapshot she had of baby Victoria. It had been taken by a friendly nurse who was trying out her new little box camera soon after the birth, and against the rules she had handed over this tiny grey likeness to Deborah. It was just a smudgy print of a little face wrapped in a shawl, but precious beyond belief.

Deborah, watching, could hardly believe what she was seeing. Her father looked at it, made a move to touch it and then withdrew his hand as though he had been stung.

At first, when she saw him reach out towards it she had wanted to spring between him and the photograph ready to snatch it away from him should he dare to pick it up, but now, as she saw him recoil, tears sprang to her eyes. They were never far from the surface lately.

They were both silent for a time and Deborah could feel her heart beating a tattoo of panic. But her father brushed aside the moment of embarrassment and stood up as if to go, to resume his ordinary life with no problems to interfere with his carefully maintained composure.

'We only live once, Deborah,' he said. 'It's about time a bit of laughter came into this house. It's what your mother would have wanted.'

'Laughter?' Deborah's self-control broke again, and she picked up the little photograph and held it in both her hands. 'How can I laugh and feel happy without my baby? How can I laugh not knowing where Victoria is, even if she's still alive?'

He held the door handle and looked at her sternly. 'Of course she's still alive.

I've recently made some inquiries. They'll soon be finding a good home for her, and then we'll know for sure. She'll be better off than back here with us. I did it only for her good.'

'What do you mean, made inquires? Why didn't you tell me?' she screamed. Indignation rose within her as well as anger.

'Mabel asked me to find out,' he said.

'Mabel?' Deborah was surprised now as well as angry. 'So you've told her all about everything have you? And what does she think of your cruelty?'

Her father twisted his hands together anxiously. 'I don't think she wholly agreed with me.'

It took a minute or so for Deborah to digest this information. The unknown Mabel sounded slightly more acceptable. Perhaps she might have a mellowing effect on her stubborn father.

'Pity you didn't listen to her then,' she said.

'It was too late,' he said as if this was

the end of the matter. Then he changed the subject. 'Her husband was killed in the blitz at the beginning of the war. He was a fireman. She has two grown up boys in the forces. She's just a friend, Deborah, but she cheers me, helps me cope with your mother's loss and with everything.'

Deborah stared at him. He suddenly looked very old and pathetic and she was surprised at the feelings of affection she still had for him. He seemed desperate for her approval.

'Would you meet her, Debbie? I know you'd like her.'

Deborah was still shocked out of her mind but the fact that this woman knew about Victoria and had even cared enough to ask about her, gave her pause for thought. Yes, she felt lonely, had need of a friendly female smile now and then.

She shrugged. 'Well, perhaps I'll try,' she said reluctantly.

'Your mother would approve. I know she would.' He smiled for the first time that evening and left the room. Deborah heard him go down the creaking stairs and felt just as shell shocked as the men she had seen from the terrible trenches of the awful first great war.

Her hands were shaking and she felt hot and cold by turns, but for now anyway, thoughts of rushing out of this house for ever would have to wait. It was still a possibility, but she would see Mabel first. This unknown woman would be the deciding factor.

Perhaps? That wonderful little word set her thinking. Could Mabel be an ally, was Victoria adopted yet? Was it all final? She would try to find out.

* * *

It was a week later that her father broached the subject of his new friend again. He would like to bring Mabel round. Deborah had been dreading this meeting and yet it was something she had to do and she wanted to get it over with. She decided to be co-operative. All her endeavours to find out where Victoria was had so far failed. How had her father managed to trace her? What did Mabel know? Meeting this unknown woman might be a first step to? To what? She tried not to hope too much.

'OK then, Dad. If you must.'

He nodded his head. 'Thanks, Debbie. You won't be disappointed. Mabel is very pleasant.'

Pleasant? She wondered what that truly meant. Well, food would break the ice.

'She'll want something to eat?' she said. It was more a question than a statement. She hoped her father would say no.

'Thank you.' He had never looked or sounded so humble. Deborah thought it was a nice change. 'I suppose I could cook supper,' she said unwillingly.

'I hadn't expected that much, but if you could I'm sure Mabel would be pleased. Just something simple.'

Deborah thought of her mother, could almost hear her voice in the quiet room. Would she want this? She stared at the grandfather clock ticking the moments away in the corner. It was her mother's treasure, this clock.

Would she be pleased to have another woman winding it every week? And in her place here at the table? Perhaps she would. She had seemed to love her husband and wouldn't want him to grieve for too long.

But Deborah wondered if she herself could possibly see another woman in her place, for that was what it might come to in the end. She shivered. Then she thought of all the unhappiness she herself had caused for both of her parents.

'All right, Dad,' she managed. 'I'll do supper of some sort if I can stretch the rations. I suppose I'd better meet her.'

Mabel was friendly and very jolly, and in spite of herself Deborah found that she warmed to her. The evening went well and when her father left to walk his friend home, Deborah knew that she had not seen him so content for a long time.

She was even feeling a little happier too. There had been no time to talk to her alone, and anyway, it was too soon. Every night in her prayers Deborah knelt and asked that no adoption had been arranged yet. But time was surely running out. She became more and more desperate.

The days passed in quick succession and a little measure of happiness returned to the terrace house, but Deborah still couldn't rid herself of her grief and anxiety, and her perpetual anger with her father.

She tried hard not to show this anger because she felt that her mother wouldn't wish it, but it was always hard to smile when she served him his meals. She knew that she should make interested queries about his working day or about the latest news of the war, but she didn't want to talk to him.

Victoria's tiny face always came between them.

His new contentment now that he was walking out with Mabel brought Deborah a small amount of relief. He wasn't at home so much and when he was, he seemed to be in a world of his own. She began to realise that this new arrangement might eventually give her freedom to live her own life again. Her father's new interest in his life might be a good thing for all of them if only she could accept it gracefully.

The news from the wireless each evening brought some cheer as well. The Russians were in Berlin, there was no hope for Hitler now, and the war was nearly over. Deborah could hardly believe it. She could scarcely remember what it was like to live in peacetime.

All her growing-up had been done while the war raged all over Europe, over most of the world in fact. She had seen terrible air-raids on Bristol, had worried about her cousins in the forces, and there was Warren fighting his way through France and Germany. If he was still alive of course! The thought of his death haunted her dreams.

But summer was coming, a summer of sunshine, longer days, and peacetime! And Mabel! One bright April day while her father was out watching a first cricket game at the County Ground there was a knock at the door, and when Deborah opened it, there was Mabel standing outside smiling at her, a little smile, an unsure smile.

'Dad's not in,' Deborah said.

'It's you I want to see, dear,' Mabel said.

'Come in.' Deborah had not been in Mabel's company on her own before and wondered what they could talk about.

Mabel followed her to the kitchen and put a large parcel on the kitchen able. 'It's material,' she said. 'Some curtains I had before the war, before the blackout. They were quite new when I had to take them down and put up all that awful black stuff. I washed them the other day and suddenly thought they'd make new dresses. My sewing machine's packed up and I wondered . . . ' She finished lamely, obviously thinking now that perhaps she shouldn't have made this rather forward suggestion to this still grieving girl.

But Deborah had been feeling lonely, was intrigued, and smiled encouragingly. 'Can I see?'

Mabel fumbled with the string and brown paper and when she had opened the parcel and spread out the contents she gasped with delight.

'It's lovely, and what a lot! Mum's sewing machine is over there.' She pointed to the old Singer treadle in the corner of the room. 'Do you want to borrow it or could we make it up here?'

'It might be better to make it here, if that's all right. There's enough for two dresses at least. One for each of us if you wanted it.'

Deborah handled the material which was a soft cotton in a peachy colour with a tiny flower pattern. She laughed. 'We wouldn't have to wear them both at the same time,' she said. 'But yes please. I wondered how I was going to manage a new dress. I haven't many coupons left for summer.'

Deborah and Mabel worked happily together on the dresses for the next few days, and when May brought Victory in Europe Day they both danced in the Bristol streets with everyone else. They decided to wear their new dresses with pride not worrying about the material being the same. 'Curtains,' they chorused when anyone grinned at them.

'And what will you use now that we can take down the blackout ones?' a neighbour asked good humouredly.

'I hadn't thought of that,' Mabel said. 'I don't think we need coupons for curtain material though do we? I'll buy some new ones.' In the general air of jollity and excitement, curtain material seemed a very small problem indeed.

It was on that jolliest of nights that Deborah first broached the subject of her baby. Mabel put her hand on her arm. 'Just tonight and tomorrow, Deborah,' she said. 'Leave it to me if you can.'

Then they whirled away into another dance and no more was said. Deborah was beside herself with questions, but every time she tried to talk about it, Mabel put her finger on her lips and wouldn't be drawn, and with that she had to be content.

Later that night there were bonfires and fireworks, and the next day street parties were arranged for the children.

'How about you and me making a few victory cakes?' Mabel said, and although food rations were small they combined what they had and made twenty little buns decorated with red, white and blue icing sugar on the top of each one. In spite of herself Deborah found that she was laughing with Mabel over their preparation, and she had to admit that Mabel had been a good thing, was even becoming a friend. The mystery between them seemed to add to their companionship.

Everyone seemed to have found something to put on the tables that were set up in the middle of nearly every road for the Victory parties, and the only thing missing for Deborah, was her baby. Victoria, a Victory baby! Deborah imagined her wearing bows of red, white and blue ribbon with a little Victory bonnet perched on her head.

Such thoughts intruded into the happiness and she tried to put all of this to the back of her mind, but she had wiped away a surreptitious tear now and then.

There were other families who were sad too that day, for so many had been killed in the last terrible six years. At least her baby was alive and probably happy in some lovely foster home, hopefully not adopted finally yet. Deborah squared her shoulders and tried to banish her own despondency, for she had never been an optimist like Mabel. The problems and difficulties of life sometimes appeared to overwhelm her.

She tried to think about others, and the future for all of them, a future which promised so much now that the world was free. Almost free! There was still Japan to vanquish. There were still prison camps in the Far East and fierce fighting going on at this very moment.

Mabel had no such gloomy thoughts. Both of her boys were likely to be demobbed soon. She was a permanent optimist. 'Good fun, isn't it,' she said, not noticing the tears as she passed jelly and cakes to the children, some of them laughing and some crying with the excitement of it all.

There was a sprinkling of men in uniform amongst the parents and Deborah thought of Warren and of Luke and Simon too. Luke at least was home now and recovering, but there had been no word of Simon yet.

July brought more cheerful news and Deborah's father resumed his habit of reading the newspaper aloud at breakfast. He had given up during the past dreadful months. He even read it sometimes when Mabel was over for supper. She would laugh at him as Pamela had never dared to, and Deborah would look at her and grin privately too.

'Okinawa Falls. The Yanks have won over there,' he read one day. 'Good for them.'

Deborah gulped on her porridge. So the Yanks had won his approval again, in this great Pacific battle now. 'Twelve thousand killed in doing it,' he continued, and then looked over the top of the newspaper at Deborah, and quickly looked down again.

Deborah merely shivered and left the table. Porridge wasn't very edible after that.

Sometimes the news was merely jolly. *The lights go on again all over Britain,* the newspaper declared. 'Pull down the blackout and put up the bright stuff.' This time Deborah grinned to herself and hoped that Mabel was right when she said that curtain material was not rationed.

That night she and Mabel went down to the centre of town and looked at the Bristol shops with their lights blazing out for all to see. Once again people were making merry and dancing in the streets. Everything had been blacked out and dim for six years. Deborah could hardly remember those pre-war days when she had been little.

'What will you do for curtains?' she asked Mabel again. They were both wearing their curtain-dresses. Mabel laughed gaily. 'Have none at first,' she said. 'Won't it be jolly to put the lights on and have no ARP warden banging on the door.'

'Put those lights out,' they both chorused together, and linked arms and danced the Lambeth Walk with everyone else down Park Street.

The real end of the war came in August. The news of the first atomic bomb falling on a Japanese town and obliterating it completely filled the newspapers, and then a few days later a second bomb was dropped.

There was a subdued air around the supper table at first as Howard opened the newspaper. Then he spoke at last. 'A good thing,' he pronounced. 'It'll save thousands of our boys. Japan will surrender now.'

'I'm glad,' Mabel said with great understatement. 'This war's truly over.' And there were more parties in the streets, more celebrations, and Aunt Sarah sent a jubilant telegram to say that she'd heard that Simon was alive and would be coming home.

Deborah stared at the brief announcement and all the memories of her childhood came flooding back. They had been lucky. No member of the family had been killed.

Amidst all of this rejoicing Deborah's father made his announcement. 'Mabel and I are to be married,' he said.

Deborah was expecting it, and she was happy now for both of them. As she had got to know Mabel all her antagonism had vanished. She felt that she had a friend in this new step-mother-to-be. 'That's wonderful, Dad,' she said. 'When?'

'We thought about the beginning of September. Mabel will move in and you'll be free, Deborah. You can go on with your studies or get a job, whatever you like.'

'Thanks, Dad,' she said. 'I've already thought about it. I'll enrol for a commercial course at the Tech. Short-hand and typing stuff.' Under her breath she added, 'And please God, let me have Victoria back.' She resolved that as soon as the wedding was over she would move heaven and earth to find Victoria. Mabel had kept quite silent about her ever since that first mysterious statement.

'I want you to have your mother's things,' her father said. He went upstairs and came back with the small leather box in which her mother had kept her jewellery. 'I want you to have your mother's rings as well as her other bits and pieces.' There were traces of tears in his eyes. 'She'd want you to have them, Debbie.'

His use of her pet name brought tears to her own eyes as well and she kissed him. 'Thank you, Daddy,' she whispered. 'Thank you.'

She opened the box and touched the little baubles her mother had loved, and she knew a sudden peace in her heart. 'I know you'll be very happy with Mabel,' she whispered.

She was sure that this new marriage was going to work. Her father was changed from the morose and difficult man he had been. Mabel had worked miracles.

★ ★ ★

There was still one special miracle to come. It happened a few days after the wedding when her father and Mabel had returned from their brief honeymoon.

Deborah and Mabel were in the kitchen together preparing supper.

'There's something I want to ask you, Debbie,' Mabel said. Her voice was hesitant and Deborah looked up from the sink where she was peeling potatoes.

'Yes?'

'It's about . . . about Victoria.'

Deborah dropped the knife into the water and gripped the edge of the sink. All her enquiries had so far led to nothing. 'What about Victoria?'

'If there was any way she could be returned to us, how would you feel?'

Deborah took the knife again and stabbed at the next potato in the bowl. 'She can't be. She must have been adopted by now. I've tried to find out where she is, but everyone is secretive. They won't tell me anything.'

'That's because you are the mother, my dear,' Mabel said kindly. 'They aren't allowed to, but they'll let your father know.'

Deborah clenched her fists. Even

now she couldn't believe that anything good could happen with Victoria if her father was involved.

'Your father and I have been to the Welfare,' Mabel said. 'She's still in a foster home. No suitable family has been found for her yet.'

Deborah's heart thumped a tattoo of sudden hope. 'What are you saying?'

Mabel took both her hands in her own and looked into her eyes. 'That if you are willing, we could offer to adopt her.'

'You and Dad?' Hope flared and then died.

'Yes, me and your father. If your dear mother hadn't died when she did, that's what would have happened. They would have brought her up.'

'How do you know that? It was always a sort of wild hope, but even before I knew Mummy was so ill, I hardly dared to believe that it could happen.'

'Do you want us to do this, Deborah? Think about it. She'd know you as her big sister. I would be her Mummy.'

Deborah released herself from Mabel's kind embrace and slumped down at the kitchen table. She could hardly take it all in. 'And Dad?' she murmured. 'What does he say?' Was this all a dream? She stared at the green baize cloth covering the old table and tried to make sense of what her step-mother was saying.

'He's agreeable if you are.'

So it was that on a beautiful autumn day Victoria came home to the house from which she had so suddenly been taken. Nine months old now, a smiling happy baby with Warren's golden curls and blue eyes.

Mabel and her father had to fetch her, were required to sign all the papers, not the final adoption papers yet, they were told. That would follow in a few week's time when everything would be made final.

Deborah had to stay at home and wait. It was the most difficult hour of her life; exciting, frightening, full of expectancy and hope, but dread that something could go wrong at that last moment.

And then they were here at the front door, in the hall, in the kitchen, and Victoria was handed to her, her lovely baby, so much older than when she had parted with her.

She was smiling and gurgling and beautiful beyond belief. Deborah felt her heart brimming over with love for her, a love that must be channelled and somehow, kept incomplete.

During those first days she tried to remember that she was sister to her little girl, and always would be. Sisters loved each other didn't they? Of course they did, but it was different from mother-love. It was not the greatest of arrangements, but it was the best that could be managed, and she knew she must be grateful and happy.

But before the arrangements had been finalised her father made a surprising announcement. Victoria was in the old zinc bath beside the kitchen fire. She was enjoying splashing and playing with the celluloid duck that floated on the soapy water and Mabel, clad in white towelling apron and with another towel ready on the clothes-horse was laughing and trying to wash the blonde curls without getting soap in Victoria's eyes.

'I've changed my mind!' The words thundered into the happy scene causing Mabel nearly to lose her grip on the slippery soapy baby and Deborah to almost drop the tray of tea things she had just cleared from the table.

'I don't want any deception,' he decreed. 'I am to be her grandad, and Mabel will be her granny. I've been thinking about it. Kept me awake all last night.' He was still sitting at the table, hands spread firmly on the tablecloth. 'And you, Deborah, will be her mother. If you agree, then a formal adoption probably won't be necessary, as you are her natural mother.'

Mabel was the first to speak. 'You didn't tell me,' she said, her voice slightly accusing, but she was smiling nevertheless.

'No need. It was what you wanted secretly all the time.'

Mabel nodded. 'But how did you know that? We hadn't talked about it.'

He smiled, heaved himself from his chair, crossed the room to his new wife and kissed her gently on her cheek. 'I knew,' he said. 'You always told me I had been hard with Debbie, and I've blamed myself for lots of things. She might have been killed in that blitz, running off to London like that, just because she was afraid of my anger.'

He straightened up and looked at his daughter. 'If you'll forgive me for all that, I'll try to make it up to you. I can't forgive myself, but perhaps having Victoria as your very own will help.'

Deborah could hardly believe what she was hearing. Her father who had been so ashamed of her pregnancy was now accepting it openly. With his love and protection, and with Mabel's love too she knew she could cope with the prejudices and ill will of those who believed that to have a baby born out of wedlock was a shame and a disgrace.

She put the tray back on the table and threw her arms around her father, the first time that she could remember doing such a thing for a very long time. 'Oh, Dad, that's wonderful.'

Then she turned to Mabel and her baby and wiped the tears from her eyes. 'Do you mind?' she said. 'Not being Mummy?'

Mabel smiled and, still holding the now protesting baby firmly she reached out for her step-daughter.

'Of course not, Debbie-love. Your dad was right. He knew that it was what I really wanted although I didn't say much about it because I was so afraid that he'd change his mind altogether. But he's right. This is the right thing to do. No lies and no deceits.'

She turned back to the baby and lifted her out of the water and wrapped her in the warm fluffy towel. 'We'll have the best of both worlds, you and me, and Victoria too. I'll look after her. After my noisy boisterous lads I'll be pleased to have a little Shirley Temple, golden ringlets and all, for my granddaughter. You can go and do your shorthand and typing, and whatever you want with your life, but you'll be Mummy always.'

Deborah looked in wonder at her step-mother. Mabel stood up and held out the baby to her. She took the wriggling little body into her arms and lowered herself carefully into the large armchair before the fire.

She kissed the damp curls but her tears fell on to them and she wiped them away along with the bath water. And she heard, in her imagination, another voice, 'She's a real swell kid, Debbie-honey.'

Then she put her hand briefly into her pocket and felt the letter there that she had received this morning. No-one else knew about it yet, and she blushed with pleasure and with hope.

She knew that the only thing she wanted to make her happiness complete was Warren here with his arms around the two of them, and since the postman had handed her the envelope with its bright foreign stamp it wasn't such a forlorn hope after all.

THE END

We do hope that you have enjoyed reading this large print book.

Did you know that all of our titles are available for purchase?

We publish a wide range of high quality large print books including:
Romances, Mysteries, Classics
General Fiction
Non Fiction and Westerns

Special interest titles available in large print are:
The Little Oxford Dictionary
Music Book, Song Book
Hymn Book, Service Book

Also available from us courtesy of Oxford University Press:
Young Readers' Dictionary
(large print edition)
Young Readers' Thesaurus
(large print edition)

For further information or a free brochure, please contact us at:
Ulverscroft Large Print Books Ltd.,
The Green, Bradgate Road, Anstey,
Leicester, LE7 7FU, England.
Tel: (00 44) **0116 236 4325**
Fax: (00 44) **0116 234 0205**

A HEART DIVIDED

Sheila Holroyd

Life is hard for Anne and her father under Cromwell's harsh rule, which has reduced them from wealth to poverty. When tragedy strikes it looks as if there is no one she can turn to for help. With one friend fearing for his life and another apparently lost to her, a man she hates sees her as a way of fulfilling all his ambitions. Will she have to surrender to him or lose everything?

SAFE HARBOUR

Cara Cooper

When Adam Hawthorne with his sharp suit and devastating looks drives into the town of Seaport, Cassandra knows he's dangerous. Not only do his plans threaten to ruin her successful harbourside restaurant, but also Adam stirs painful memories she'd rather forget. When Cassandra's sister Ellie turns up, in trouble as usual, Cassandra needs all her considerable strength to cope. But will discovering dark secrets from Adam's past change Cassandra's future? And will he be her saviour or her downfall?

THE HAPPY HOSTAGE

Charles Stuart

When an agreement is made with the U.S.A. to build missile bases in Carmania, Elisabeth Renner and her friends plot to kidnap the American ambassador to Carmania and force the agreement to be cancelled. However, they get the wrong man: Charles Gresham, a budding British business tycoon. And he soon finds himself sympathising with his pretty captor. Then Elisabeth reluctantly decides to call it all off, and things really go wrong — when Charles doesn't want to be released!

STILL THE ONE

Joan Reeves

Ally Fletcher fights her way through a torrential downpour to Mr Burke Winslow and his bride at their marriage ceremony! Ally's arrival at the church halts the nuptials when she delivers her bombshell: the groom is already married — to her! However, this businessman isn't in love: he needs a wife for two weeks, purely for financial reasons. Anyone will do — even his insufferable ex. Soon Burke and Ally are temporarily reliving their disastrous marriage — and their sensational, sizzling honeymoon . . .

LESSONS IN LOVE

Chrissie Loveday

1963. Lucy's first teaching job turns out to be more than she bargained for . . . fired with enthusiasm to show her teaching skills, she is brought down to earth when she faces a depressing room and difficult pupils. However, her mum is always there for her and she soon begins to find herself with an increasingly complicated love life. Who should she choose to spend time with? And why is the Headmaster so concerned about the company she keeps?